UNREMEMBERED VICTORY

TIME FOR THIS WAR STORY TO BECOME AMERICAN HISTORY

Dennis H. Klein

ISBN: 978-0-692-17595-8

Printed in the United States of America

Contents

TESTIMONIALS

Simon Green, Abrams Artist Agency
Unremembered Victory is an extraordinary story full of heroism and a piece of history that I never heard about. Mr. Klein writes from the heart and much of this really propels the reader forward.

Sid Ganis, Hollywood Producer
Klein is an extraordinary writer. Not at all self-conscious. Puts it all out there. His passion for this is crystal clear. Altogether a pretty amazing story. Read it TWICE. The eyewitness account about the 200 high school students was fascinating. He should take a crack at the screenplay.

5 Star Amazon Review
Vincent H. May 6, 2019
I served in Korea during the war and have always been interested in action taken after my departure. On occasion I heard stories of firefights, an overview with few details. This book is excellent, it tells the unbiased stories of those serving on the DMZ. I can understand what these men went through. Like the Forgotten War those serving on the DMZ were forgotten. These men suffered bitter cold, fire fights and the effects of Agent Orange. This is a story that must be told. It is history and should be taught to the young of today. God Bless them!

5 Star Amazon Review
By W. MacQuoid on September 6, 2018
Just bought this fresh out book. It is part of my history having served there about that time. MP guard on Freedom Bridge looking out on the DMZ. 100% Agent Orange Disabled Veteran.

5 Star Amazon Review
F Davis on September 11, 2018
"Unremembered Victory" is a true account of the DMZ War in Korea. I'm happy to see that this story has been written. Every family needs to have a copy in their personal library. This story needs to be shared with the younger generation since there is no mention of it in our history books. I encourage you to purchase a copy for your personal library.

5 Star Amazon Review

Lance Atchley September 12, 2018

I rated this book 5 stars because the story needs to be told and retold. Having served in the same unit from 1972 to 1974, I recall hearing this history while assigned there. My thanks to Dennis for his service and writing this story!

5 Star Amazon Review

Marve E Lus On June 4, 2019

Thought it a great perspective view on what went on in South Korea during the time. Served there contemporary to the story but was assigned to higher Headquarters at I Corps commanding both the 2nd ID and the 7th ID. In G2 I spent much of my time all along the DMZ on ground, mountain tops, and in the air doing reconnaissance. During my time in the TOC incursions, firefights, armistice violations where frequent and never ending. The book reflects the spirit of the front-line men who were on the line and very much fighting with as much intensity as could be. Good read brought a sense of nostalgia to me as at the time I was very young and remembered it and could sense the authenticity.

4 Star Amazon Review

Vincent H on May 24, 2019

I served in Korea during the war and have always been interested in action taken after my departure. On occasion I heard stories of firefights, an overview with few details. This book is excellent, it tells the unbiased stories of those serving on the DMZ. I can understand what these men went through. Like the Forgotten War those serving on the DMZ were forgotten. These men suffered bitter cold, fire fights and the effects of Agent Orange. This is a story that must be told. It is history and should be taught to the young of today. God Bless them!

Bernard Catalonato,
Mill Valley CA.
Unremembered Victory is a mindblower. I've heard some of these stories, but it was only when I could read them in one go that I could understand the importance of Korea 1968. This is an American war story told in the spirit of Hemingway's Farewell to Arms and Mailer's Naked and the Dead, in an intense style that evokes Thomas Wolfe and Dave Eggers. It's an E-ticket; enjoy the ride.

Eddy K., Veteran
I enjoyed reading the book Unremembered Victory by Dennis H. Klein. Having served in Vietnam I related to the danger and fear associated with service in the Korean DMZ. I recommend for the public to learn the truth from that era.

Brent M.
In the book Unremembered Victory, I really liked the way musical lyrics were used illustrating the times. I had not known the story of the Korean HOSTILITIES and the story is educational.

Bob Cranston, Mill Valley CA
Klein's Unremembered Victory presents its readers with a serious premise and, concurrently, a call to rally to a cause of action on behalf of our country. This is a romp through a war never reported so as not to confuse the ONE STORY of the 60s Generation allowed by mainstream press— Vietnam. I agree with the author that this is a SECOND STORY to Nam that convinces us that we are better than we are told. It is a '68 story how we started the year STILL unabashedly believing in Truth Justice and the American Way. Due the excesses of Vietnam, by the end of the year we did not know what we believed in and still don't. Being better than we are told is intended to replace the current need to offset pain of being an American by feeling superior to others with believing in one another again.

Vernon S. Veteran
Unremembered Victory a good read. Interesting commentary on the General but hard ass, hands off or hands on, but he did know and care what was going on in the Division I think,

Bill S, Veteran
Unremembered Victory a story that needs to be publicized though I fear no one cares anymore. I can promise one thing I will fight for all the KIA of the 2nd KOREAN WAR to receive the recognition and honor they deserve.

INTRODUCTION

UNREMEMBERED VICTORY,
THE 2ND KOREAN WAR AS IT HAPPENED
ALONG THE AMERICAN SECTOR OF THE
KOREAN DIMILITARIZED ZONE

Unremembered Victory is a war story about four thousand nobody accidental unknown heroes of an unreported war along the Korean DMZ, never acknowledged for saving the world from a nuclear ending in 1968. All the events in it are, or are accepted as, true. Sources are of three types. 1) Interpretation of official records. 2) Hearsay of eyewitness accounts. 3) Primarily real-time eye-witness recollections of two main characters. One is an officer who was on the Line by day but slept south of the DMZ at night. The other is a Sergeant (Non-Commissioned Officer) who was on the Line, night and day. IF you are not versed about this period of American history, you are urged to first read a brief official account of the DMZ War in 'Fighting Brush Fires on Korea's DMZ' by Richard K. Kolb at the permission of VFW Magazine, APPENDIX A

How are so many details so clear to the author after 50 years? Spend enough time in the DMZ north of the Anti-Infiltration Fence in '68, essentially a free-fire zone, and you never really leave. Accounts of what happened out there just get more intense and sweeter when compared to the rest of your life. Though the author met GIs who were later killed or wounded, they were fortunately only faces in the crowd to him. None were close enough to cause 'survivor's remorse', a root cause of PTSD suffered by many DMZ War vets to this day. This is further complicated by these 'officially ordinary' GIs having never been thanked or acknowledged for not letting the world go nuclear so our children could be born. Though the author faced the fire many times, to assure eye-witness validity of lethal combat, contributions from the above mentioned Sargent 'who was there' has been stitched into the overall thread of events. The Acknowledgements Section tells more about the service of this contributor, a member of the most forwardmost infantry unit in the DMZ during the same time as the author was on the Line.

All characters are based on people who the author served with during his 21-month tour of Korea. Poetic license is everywhere. Many speeches are fabricated as accurately as possible from official records. Words said by one are put into the mouths of another. Timelines are adjusted to create drama. Overall, this book is intended to be the most accurate portrayal as possible of what happened out there. Read about the 4000 hapless US GIs who were all that stood in the way of oblivion.

A most interesting aspect of this victory is that of the 4,000 on the Line, all were selected by the Pentagon out of the US Army ranks using a Monte Carlo computer routine that randomly chose from among the millions in service only those in the middle of the bell curve of capability. This filtered out the high-end, all in Vietnam to make rank, and the low-end who only went to Nam. If it was an experiment, it was a success. Hence if any randomly selected 4,000 'qualified' Vietnam GIs were swapped in for the 4,000 GIs on the DMZ, the result would have been the same. The ordinary among us is enough because that's who we are.

Read about the 4,000 and come to believe in the 4000. Read some more and realize that since the whole lot of them were officially ordinary, know that you too could be, at least, one of them. Learn how, this being a 'right fight' you would gladly face the fire and even be ready to take the hit for all the right reasons. This book was written to give back to everyone a modicum of the unifying force of an honorable military history, something to hold on to adrift in a manufactured sea of dread and distrust spawned by fifty years of shameful wars starting with Vietnam. Unremembered Victory offers up to you the oh so ordinary 4,000 on the Line in the Winter of '68 compelling evidence that WE ARE ALL A WHOLE LOT BETTER THAN WE ARE TOLD.

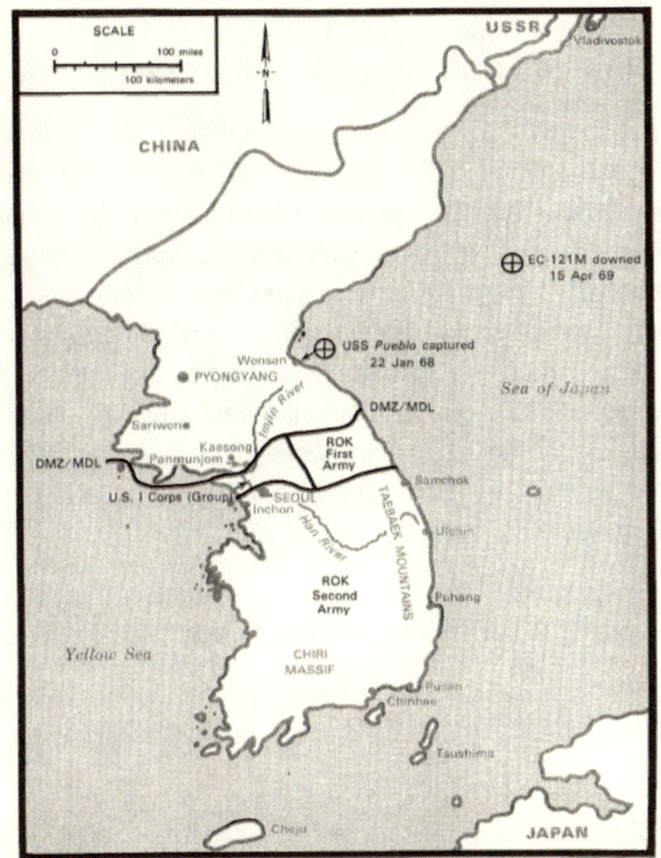

SOURCE: Scenes from an Unfinished War: Low-Intensity Conflict in Korea, 1966–1969 Paperback – January 1, 2011 by Daniel P. Bolger, Combat Studies Institute

NOTE: For an in-depth official record of the 2nd Korean War read the above reference.

http://smallwarsjournal.com/documents/unfinishedwarkorea.pdf

Dennis H. Klein

1

NOW INCLUDES EVERYTHING UP UNTIL NOW

On a dark January night in 1968, two GIs were in a small fortification along the Anti-Infiltration Fence (AIF) that cuts across the Korean Demilitarized Zone (DMZ). One was asleep down in the dugout at the bottom of this position. The other was watching North Korean commandoes cutting holes in the AIF and slipping through, one after the other. The weather was bitter cold, dreary, dark. The wind was howling. Snow covered the ground. The Fence that stretched across the entire Korean Peninsula disappeared out of sight to the east and west. The GI, in full winter gear, intently looking forward, woke up his partner and whispered, "Hey! Wake up. Holy shit. Look. They're coming through the Fence." The second GI whispered, "WTF. How many of them?"

The first GI whispered, "WTF, at least 10 are already through and they just keep coming. A bunch of them and they're armed."

The second GI whispered, "Wow. So many and just the two of us. We can't take them on alone. You have to call this in right away and ask for help."

The first GI motioned both to descend into the dugout where their whispers, for sure, could not be overheard. "I already tried," said the first soldier, "I could not get the phone to work. BIG SURPRISE. Hell, nothing around here works. The phone and everything else are the same gear they were using in '53 at the end of the Korean War. Damn, damn, damn! Now we sit here with a phone that does not work when we need it most. Here. You give it a try."

The second GI whispers, "Let's see? I remember the ON switch is here and… HOLY SHIT, the battery is dead!"

" Don't look at me. I only work here." whispered the first GI. "Nam gets the gravy and we get the grinds, all this antiquated junk."

'Hey! Consider ourselves lucky! Have you heard the sound it makes when you turn it on? Better it's dead. It's so loud; no way these guys would not hear it and we would soon be as dead as these batteries."

                                    Unremembered Victory

The first GI whispers, "Quiet. I'm going back up and see what they're up to." As seen over the sandbags, he exclaimed, "Holy shit, this is bad. There must be at least 20 standing around now. They are just milling about, waiting as even more come through."

A commando stopped and looked in their direction. Pausing, he whispered to one of the other commandos, who shook his head and looked elsewhere. This first commando looked again, and he too looked away.

The first GI whispered, "If we fire on them, there are so many, we won't last a second."

The second GI whispered, "I say we hunker down in the bottom of this hole and let them go on their way, and we will be safe until they are gone."

The first GI whispered, "Amen to that."

Now a total of 31 commandos stood in plain sight through a misty moonlit night, but only as shadowy forms of bodies shrouded in coveralls over their South Korean Army uniforms beneath. These are not ordinary North Korean Army soldiers. They are not the usual specially trained elite North Korean infiltrators, typically sons of the Party Elite, assigned to the North Korean side of the DMZ. No. Referred to as Group 124 by the North Koreans, they were commandos of possibly the highest order. To this day, the US Marines study the curriculum behind their most rigorous training program, turning out perhaps the most lethal fighting force ever in the field with just hand-held weapons.

The second GI whispers, "Look. They are starting to move southeast and won't pass close to us. So, once they were out of sight, I'll go on foot to the Lieutenant and let him know what happened." The first GI whispers "Are you crazy? Figure it out. If we tell the Lieutenant what happened, we could be brought up on charges for letting it happen."

The first GI whispers, "Letting it happen, Now you're crazy? What could we have done but get killed trying to stop them? The real problem is the damn phone is dead. Hell, nothing works around here. Nothing gets fixed. Has anyone ever tested it? No. First time we need to use it and it's a dud. Blame it on the phone. We could not call in support and, sure as hell, could not have done it on foot without getting killed. Better we're still here to fight another day."

The second GI whispers, "Hey. Someone else will spot them and call it in. WTF does this have to do with you or me anyway? Just keep it to ourselves? What do ya' say. promise?"

The first GI whispers emphatically, "Promise!"

THE FOOL ON THE HILL
Beatles

Day after day alone on the hill,
The man with the foolish grin Is keeping perfectly still,
But nobody wants to know him, they can see that he's just a fool,
And he never gives an answer, But the fool on the hill
Sees the sun going down, And the eyes in his head,
See the world spinning around.

2
YOU CANNOT MAKE ANYONE DO ANYTHING,
BUT YOU CAN CHANGE WHAT IT IS THEY WANT TO BELIEVE

What happened that night was the kick-off of The DMZ War, as named by the Army War College. It started out looking like so many other 1968 bad news stories, full of humiliation, injustice, obscenity and defeat, like one tragic wave after another breaking on the beach of our conscious-ness. However, what is described here is perhaps the ONE good news story of 1968, one full of grace, honor and triumph but for reasons to be explored has never been made part of our history.

As just stated, this war did not start well. The low morale of those two GIs who let the commandos go was systemic throughout the ranks, spawned by nothing to do for the last 15 years since the Korean War ended. Suddenly, out of nowhere, it's all about the Line holding against vastly superior forces.

For those who may not remember and those who do, 1968 starts off with the Vietnam War taking a dive with the Tet Offensive, a humiliating defeat of the US Military. Amassing great secret stores of hidden ammo and weapons, the North Vietnamese launched highly coordinated nation-wide lethal attacks on US forces at the end of January. Overrunning American installations everywhere ended the American manufactured myth of winning a 'War of Attrition'. American losses grew to a record 509 killed in action (KIA) in a single week in February.

Right in the middle of Tet, Martin Luther King's assassination sparked lethal race riots across LA, Chicago, Washington DC and Detroit. With the Soviets successfully gaining ever more ground in Asia, Africa, and Latin America, in May world opinion was dragged further to the Russian camp by the semi-communist student movements of the Paris 4th Com-munard. In June, Bobby Kennedy was assassinated as a run-up to the Democratic Chicago Convention mass head bashing. This was closely followed by the lethal clearing of student demonstrators from the streets in front of the '68 Mexican Olympics. Three hundred were killed by the police (many from upper crust families) in what was to become known as "The Tlatelolco Massacre." The opening ceremonies followed 2 days later as though nothing had happened. In August, a deadly Russian tank Invasion abruptly ended Prague Spring, Czechoslovakia's early effort to elude Soviet control. Worst of all, as the year came to an end, a grim truth crept across the American people: We are going to lose a war.

Hidden under all this debris was a singular good-news story about 4,000 US Army GIs on the Korean DMZ suddenly in the way of 380,000 combat ready Korean People's Army soldiers bent on invading South Korea. Not to worry! This tale has a nuclear option. Everyone in the ranks was under orders that upon invasion they were to make the greatest number of enemy soldier's mass up on top of them by refusing to retreat even one foot. What would happen after being overrun was, according to your security clearance, different versions of everyone being nuked. While Vietnam tipped forever into the abyss, 3,000 miles to the north, the US Army fights its way to an unremembered victory. 'Victory', because America unconditionally won a lethal game of Cold War chicken—the enemy blinked first giving up any notion of taking over South Korea. 'Unremembered'. Have you seen the movie or read the popular book? This story is too big to drop out of history for lack of mainstream media coverage.

So how is a draw a victory? George F. Kennon RULES on this one. His unanimously adopted belief that containment was enough to end the the Soviet Union proved oh so true. Keep the spoils of expansion funding the inevitable systemic corruption and Communism collapses in on itself.

To date, the one story of our generation has been only Vietnam. This is a second story to Nam that happened at the same time as the Tet Offensive in January 1968 but has never made the popular media. You have heard over and over that it would have been different if Vietnam had been the 'right fight'. This is a real-time story about what it was like when a bunch of ordinary American soldiers found themselves in such a fight.

Now flash forward to Seoul in 2016 – everywhere this modern-day first world city shows off over-the-top soaring office and condo complexes and tasteful, if not daring, municipal buildings with art and design present everywhere. At a wedding reception, the revelers are mostly Korean, juxtaposed with a splattering of American friends and family of the groom. There was light banter as the Korean father of the bride toasts the newlyweds. Gangnam Style music can be heard from afar.

The father of the bride toasts, "To my radiant daughter and my new son: may only the best come to you all of your days."

The next speaker is Daniel Schikevitz, nephew of the groom. This is his second time in Korea, the first time was a 21 Month tour as a US Army Combat Engineer officer. During the whole two weeks of this revisit to Korea, he could not stop thinking about his days on the Line and phenomenal modernization that had followed. Well he could remember the drive north out of Seoul in '68. He remembered there was no electricity 5 miles out of Seoul to the DMZ, occasional 2 story crude concrete buildings lined the road housing shops. In between were the ubiquitous rice farming villages composed of a few score thatch houses clustered together upslope from shared rice paddies. On the road were only trucks, buses, a spattering of cars and lots of donkey, and even human-drawn, carts on this dusty two-lane unpaved link between Seoul and the DMZ - two dirt lanes wide enough for easy passing. That was it. After the wedding, Dan had visited the DMZ where he was assigned back in '67– '69. The journey began in a highly contemporary subway that did not daylight until over halfway to the Imjin River, southern extent of the DMZ. Everywhere, Dan saw precisely built infrastructure impeccably maintained. The only time Dan could remember a train ride that smooth was in Scotland.

Then he saw it. No more villages. No more dirt roads. No more rice paddies. All in under 50 years had been replaced by ultra-modern condo complexes, elegant towering office buildings, topped by a most spectacular commercial center looking right into North Korea that would make Century City in Beverly Hills blush.

Daniel toasted the bride saying: "As uncle of the groom, I congratulate you and your family on your success and the outrageous success the entire Korean people in what you have achieved in such a short time. Please let me say again words I heard so long ago." Daniel paused and held his wine glass high and easily declared,

"Mighty and great are the Korean People!"

Everyone applauds.

Daniel enjoyed a sentiment shared by many DMZ Veterans with a lot of time on the Line. Like a perk, happy were the recollections of absolute meaning when everything added up. Under orders, combat zone, facing the fire, weapon at the ready, safety off, finger on trigger, ready to take the hit in that eternal struggle between free will and constraint.

PEOPLE GOT TO BE FREE
The Rascals

All the world over, so easy to see
People everywhere just wanna be free
Listen, please listen, that's the way it should be
Peace in the valley, people got to be free

You should see, what a lovely, lovely world this would be
If everyone learned to live together
It seems to me such an easy, easy thing this would be
Why can't you and I learn to love one another

3
WHEN EXISTENCE IS MY ONLY WITNESS,
I'M IN GOOD COMPANY

In a forested area near a hilltop overlooking Seoul below, at dusk, four brothers out cutting firewood stumble across the commandos hunkered down in an encampment. The first commando to see them said, "Sir. Look what just wandered into camp. These four. They say they are all brothers."

Puzzled, the commando Commander said, "We have a problem. We got all the way here without being detected and now this."

The first commando affirmed, "I say we kill them now that they've seen us."

Due to the muffled tone of the commando voices too low to hear the actual words, the four brothers started thinking their future may not be much longer, and the oldest brother nods to the others and said to the commandos, "We are so glad you have come. We have waited so long to be liberated from our dictator leader keeping us from being free under Communism."

The Commander declared, "Absolutely! We live for the day that all of Korea is one nation under Communism."

The eldest brother blurted, "Thanks for coming to save us."

The Commander declared, "Okay. Okay. Better to have you live for the cause. So, do I have your word that you will tell ABSOLUTELY NO ONE that you saw us?"

Brother One said, "Yes. You can count on us. Let us be on our way so you can be on yours to what you must do to make all of Korea one again. The commando Commander then said with a wink, "How would you like it if we killed President Park? Would that speed things up?"

All four brothers in unison declared quite loudly, "We hate President Park. Go do it!"

The Brothers packed up and left the scene quite quickly. Upon their departure, the Commander concluded, "I don't really trust them, but remember, our plan is to go into Seoul in groups of threes and fours. IF they have an inkling that we are coming, they will be looking for 20 or more together. Check your maps. Each group has a different route. We rendezvous at the Sunga's Temple. It is on the highest ground so you can use it like a target. We disperse wide and converge at exactly 4:00 PM. (1600 hours). Okay. Form your teams and take off. See you at Sunga's."

At the same time, hundreds of miles to the south, a group of some 100 high school students were in formation doing calisthenics in a flat dirt school yard. They had a look of youthful hope and promise in their bright, ironed white and black school uniforms, despite a seamless sea of poverty that stretched everywhere. These were nice kids, village kids, living in traditional hamlet style clusters of earth walled and thatch roof huts, but up on the times just the same, their village being quite close to Pusan, the second largest metro in Korea after Seoul. They disperse from the formation and playfully leave the school yard. A quick look at their young faces indicates a certain edge about them. True, they come off like a bunch of happy kids, but not far from this moment is their frustration with curfews every night, the chance of getting abducted or killed in abortive commando raids. They were sick of all the check points and sick of cowering all the time, humiliated by the North Korean infiltrators constantly disrupting the public order.

Meanwhile, the four brothers left the commandos and ran directly to a provincial police station. There was a lot of clamor inside, until finally an older police official entered the room and sat down at a desk. Whereupon Brother One said, "We stumbled onto a bunch of North Korean soldiers while cutting wood. At first, they were going to kill us and then we used the trick we were taught in our village. We acted like we were glad to be liberated and a lot of other stuff and they let us go."

The cop barked, "How many were there?"

The eldest brother hesitated, "Unless I missed one, there were 31 in all."

The Police Commandant enquired, "That's quite a force. What do you think they are up to?"

The eldest brother mirthfully stated, "Once they thought we were loyal to their cause, like a joke, they said they were out to kill President Park to

                                   Unremembered Victory

speed the day we are once again a united Korea. We further convinced them to let us go by earnestly saying we hated President Park, the only words of truth we spoke. Village training good. Telling them what they want to hear saved our life."

The cop added, "You may have saved a lot more lives than you know."

At this same moment, one group of four commandos was running through a full climax oak forests like fawns, under a dense canopy, with no understory to encumber their progress. Down and through the steep majestic uninhabited north-south trending ridges they ran from the DMZ to Seoul. At the same time, a second set of five ran through a different wooded area. Another team of five, having reached urban areas, commenced to rapidly walk through alleyways, looking straight ahead as they passed army and security units who were making sweeps looking for a larger group of men. Still another group of four rapidly walked into town. Repeat this scenario some six times and all 31 penetrated to downtown Seoul and converged at the huge Temple. Their Commander was subtly nodding to the incoming groups to slip into a heavily forested area next to the Temple. As each arrived, they threw off their coveralls, revealing their South Korean uniforms beneath. When all were ready, they proceeded in smart formation right past South Korean military units on alert in the streets. Their destination was in sight, The Blue House, presidential palace of Chung Hee Park, South Korea's president, who they had come to assassinate along with the US Ambassador. Just two blocks away, a policeman at a check point notices their boots aren't regulation and asks, "What is your unit?

The commando Commander barked, "The 126th Sir!"

Military Police Commander said, "What part?"

commando Commander barked again, "Regiment D."

Military Police Commander, pulling out his pistol raising it to shoot, "126th has no regiments, only Companies."

… at which point the Policeman, upon pulling out his gun, was shot dead by one of the commandos.

Even when in full retreat, some of the commandos set ambushes while others provoked their assailants to chase them, leading them right into their well placed ambush. They were more intent on being warriors first and getting home safe second. In a heavy gun fight at a street intersection, a hapless bus rolled into the crossfire resulting in the death of 22 civilians. Fighting continued all the way from downtown Seoul back to the Anti-Infiltration Fence. Only one commando got back home alive and one other was captured. Something else—while all this was going on, totally unrelated, three US Army GIs were killed north of the AIF on the same day. From then on, for months, there was no letup in fire fights all up and down the Line.

BORN TO BE WILD
Steppenwolf

Get your motor running' Head out on the highway
Lookin' for adventure and whatever comes our way
Yeah Darlin' go make it happen
Take the world in a love embrace
Fire all of your guns at once
And explode into space

4

SOME KNOW, FOR SURE, THERE IS TRUTH IN THE HILLS OTHERS CAN ONLY KNOW, FOR SURE, THERE IS TRUTH IN THE TOWNS

It was the situation room at 8th Army Headquarters. General Bonesteel said to US Ambassador Adams and Major General Frank M. Izenour, 2nd Infantry Division Commanding Officer, "Looks like after all these years of nothing happening, we have a real fight on our hands. I am pleased to say that 8th Army asked for and will soon be receiving enough men to completely fill our morning reports. But what good does that do us unless we can turn our sorry troops into something useful?"

General Bonesteel turned to General Izenour and said, "WTF happened out there. Don't answer. Right off the top you are not taking the fall alone for this mess. We knew that all over 8th Army the morale had taken 15 years of doing nothing to get this deep in the crapper. This place was unraveling more than I knew and I knew it was bad. We all did. I did not do enough and now we need you to do all that you can to make the 2ID into an Army ... FAST! Bullets are flying now, and Intelligence tells us that the North Koreans are testing our resolve to stand against invasion. We have been getting ready for this for years, so we are going to go with what we got. Since the 2nd Infantry Division is what we've got, then the 2ID will have to be enough. We all know the option to the Line not holding, so it's up to you, Frank. I am counting on you. Don't let me down."

General Izenour said, "Sir. Do I have authority over what corrective actions I choose?"

General Bonesteel snapped back, "Do whatever it takes. You have my word I will back you up."

Upon these words, General Izenour's mood became agitated, and after a second or two, all 6 foot 4 inches of his lanky Texan made overtures that he could not get started soon enough. Izenour requested, and was granted, dismissal. Whereupon, he turned on his heals and dashed out of the room.

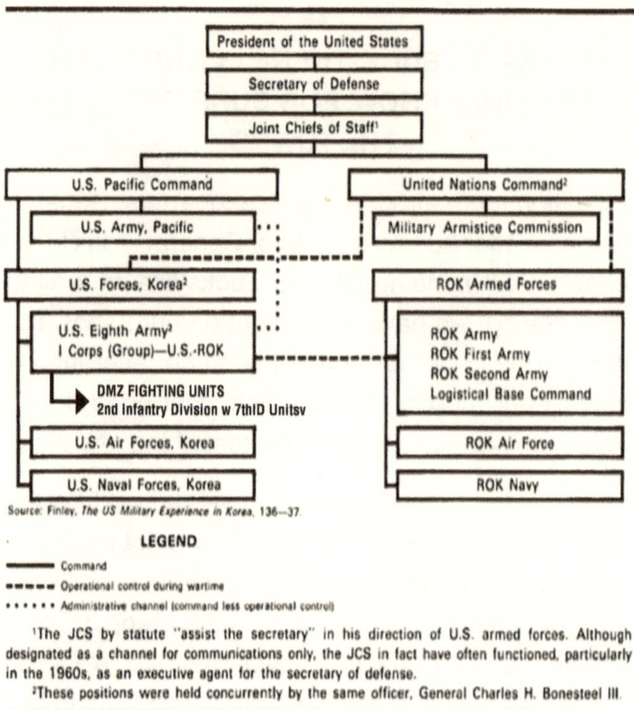

Source: Finley, *The US Military Experience in Korea*, 136—37.

LEGEND

——— Command
▬ ▬ ▬ ▬ Operational control during wartime
• • • • • • Administrative channel (command less operational control)

[1]The JCS by statute "assist the secretary" in his direction of U.S. armed forces. Although designated as a channel for communications only, the JCS in fact have often functioned, particularly in the 1960s, as an executive agent for the secretary of defense.

[2]These positions were held concurrently by the same officer, General Charles H. Bonesteel III.

After General Izenour departed, Bonesteel's Aid de-Camp went on to further brief General Bonesteel about another recent development, "Sir, we have lost the USS Pueblo, a spy ship on the high seas. According to the Pentagon, the Pueblo was far from shore, spying not on North Korea but on Russian ship movements and radio transmissions. The Pueblo was not put on alert about the Blue House commando Raid just the day before. The Pueblo was subsequently attacked without warning, surrounded by enemy ships and multiple MIG fighter jets. To buy time to destroy documents and equipment, the Pueblo pretended to cooperate with the North Koreans, but when the KPA tried to board, the Pueblos' skipper, Commander Lloyd Mark Bucher, turned the ship and tried to escape by setting out for the open sea. Way too slow to outrun the enemy gunboats, The Pueblo's deck was quickly raked by lethal fire, killing one and wounding nine. Captain Bucher let them board. The only weapons on board were two mounted 50 caliber machine guns. They were completely exposed with no armaments. Word has it that not all materials were destroyed in time, including two of the decoders on board."

                                      Unremembered Victory

The first thought by many officers upon hearing about the Pueblo was 'Betrayal'. Within a day of its capture there seemed to be a broad awakening of a masculine urge among the officers and Sergeants in the 2nd Infantry Division to look inside themselves, and then at each other, to find the resolve to believe that, when they faced lethal fire, they would do a better job than the Pueblo. At the offer's mess, a lot of the talk was about 'being ready.'

About the same time the Pueblo news broke, General Izenour was on board his Huey Helicopter flying North. Though General Bonesteel's rebuke was diplomatic, it was a reprimand just the same. General Izenour was in a complete state of rage with an intensity he knew exactly how to tap for maximum dramatic result. It was a half hour helicopter ride from downtown Seoul Korea to the DMZ. Down below, all was winter, grim, gray, poor, decrepit and bleak with sprawling hovels spreading some five miles north out of Seoul. Then the view transitioned to the countryside composed of nothing but sticks and thatch small villages nestled in the trees upslope, vegetable gardens in front. There was no electricity or phone service outside of Seoul, most of the nation was still ultra-primitive. The Huey then crossed the Imjin River and turned east along the AIF.

General Izenour soon saw exactly what he knew he was going to see; two GIs asleep with their rifles on sandbags and helmet on top to make it look like they were on duty. Instead, they dozed at the bottom of their dug-out position. General Izenour leaned over and told the pilot, "See those two GIs sleeping over there. Scoot over that way a little but land far enough away so we do not wake them up." The Helicopter landed some 200 yards from the sleeping men. General Izenour remained on board telling the pilot to get their Brigade Headquarters on the radio, and then he asked for the Brigade's Commander to join him.

Time passed, and General Izenour was fuming, getting his speech ready in his head for the hapless officer with the bad luck of being in the wrong place at the wrong time. A lone Jeep appeared on the horizon with a Bird Colonel on board who jumped out and walked toward the Helicopter. General Izenour stepped out of his Helicopter and walked toward the Colonel. The Colonel gave the General the best salute he had and General Izenour did not return the salute. The Colonel continued to salute, as General Izenour, repeatedly pointing to the two sleeping soldiers, growled at the Bird Colonel, "Normally I would chew you out for your Battalion Commander letting his Company Commander, letting his Platoon leader, letting his Squad leader, letting their men sleep on duty. However, any words of reprimand would be wasted on you since you are hereby relieved of command as of right now."

The Bird Colonel slowly dropped his salute since it had become silly to continue to offer it any longer. The bewildered Brigade Commander then asked, "But sir, If I am relieved of my command, what do you want me to do next?" to which General Izenour snapped back with a piercing scream, "I will tell you what you won't do next. You WILL NOT sleep in Korea tonight!" The Bird Colonel started to ask another question and thought better of it. Glumly, but quickly, he got back in his Jeep, and the Jeep sped away. General Izenour returned to his Huey.

ALL ALONG THE WATCHTOWER
Bob Dylan

There must be some way out of here,
Said the joker to the thief,
There's too much confusion, I can't get no relief,
Businessmen, they drink my wine, plough men dig my earth, none of
them along the Line know what any of it is worth.

"No reason to get excited," the thief, he kindly spoke,
"There are many here among us now,
Who feel that life is but a joke,
But you and I, we've been through that, and this is not our fate,
So let us not talk falsely now, the hour is getting late"

                                                            Unremembered Victory

5

"I'M THIRTY, I SAID. "I'M FIVE YEARS TOO OLD
TO LIE TO MYSELF AND CALL IT HONOR."
[THE GREAT GATSBY: F. SCOTT FITZGERALD]

While General Izenour was getting his ass kicked by General Bonesteel, 1st LT. Daniel Schikevitz, the very same person 48 years later attending his brother's son's wedding in modern day Seoul, was told to report to his superior officer, Captain McDowell, S3 Operations Officer. Like all the West Point grads along the DMZ, he graduated in the bottom third of his class, but still a guy everyone wanted to hang with, and he offered little resistance. He had all the faculties for running an effective and smooth S3 (battalion operations) shop, and he did that with a healthy detachment of having no plans of staying in the Army. The bottom of West Point was still tops in just about everything else. Thank you, USA.

Captain McDowell explained to Daniel, "As you know The Pueblo was seized on the high seas yesterday. That, combined with the Blue House Raid, gives 8th Army every reason to believe there may soon be intense action in our sector, either by an attempted North Korean invasion or a response to reprisal by us to get back the captured spy ship. Either way, the bang bang that started yesterday does not look like it's going to abate anytime soon. For that reason, 2ID is on highest alert. Since HQ considers this information too sensitive to trust to Top Secret Crypto transmission, you will deliver one of these three envelopes to A, C and Bridge Company Commanders. Each contains the coordinates of where to go and what to take to the field. Put their envelope in their hand, tell them generally what's in it and get the hell out of there so you can get this all done today. And watch out! I got Simpson as your Jeep driver. Make sure he takes extra ammo clips, and at least four grenades in the Jeep. That would be a good thing." As they parted, Captain McDowell made 'the motion' oh so subtle and kind spirited, pretending like he was throwing some sand at Daniel's feet. More about 'the motion' later.

Despite ample sounds of sporadic firefights somewhere else all up and down the Line, Daniel got to each Company Headquarters without incident. It was a cold dismal morning. Once again, the Land of the Morning calm did not disappoint. Though the air was still, like a hammer, humid cold air pounded Daniel's face and body during the half hour open top Jeep ride to Bridge Company, first on the list. Dan was okay with the damp cold, the DC Metro winter cold being a humid thing. So stoic about their own dry 30 below zero cold, oh how those Minnesota boys whined about the winter of '67 at Fort Belvoir, also in the DC Metro. On and on they complained about how nothing could keep that humid cold from getting inside their clothes and chilling them to the bone, though it was rarely below 20 above.

Daniel's dad got the American Dream right. He climbed out of the tenements and a broken home in the Richmond, Virginia to a Civil Engineering degree, to a brick bungalow, to his own construction company, to a trophy house in Bethesda and some money to spare. Daniel attended the University of Maryland, earning a Civil Engineering degree himself. Though his dad took his stand in DC, Daniel, also descended from store owners in Norfolk, Virginia on his Mom's side. As such, he spent a lot of summers parked with southern relatives where he came to believe one part of the "Southern Code" that could have done him in.

'If you don't have an honorable way out of the draft, serve or forever be a coward.'

This code was the ONLY reason Daniel went in. Otherwise, like most of the 10 million others in his cohort, Daniel's feeling was, "YOU'VE GOT TO BE KIDDDING ME! This is not a war. This is an obscenity."

Ducking a Vietnam tour and STILL winding up facing enemy fire anyway had many on the DMZ smiling to themselves all the time. Some months the casualty rate exceeded Afghanistan, but so much lighter than Vietnam. With some 100 GIs killed in '68 gave a guy on the Line one chance in 40 to be a casualty, venturing north of the Fence took manageable trepidation. The DMZ War was by many measures a 'right fight'—You served under the American and United Nations flag, fighting cheek and jowl with KATUSAs (Korean Augmentation Troops USA) in a state of near seamless mutual trust against a clear and present threat of totalitarianism determined to replace 'do what you want' with 'do what you're told.'

To die for! That's how Dan saw it as did much of his generation of free will maniacs. Drawing on some of Martin Luther King's words,

> 'IF there is nothing you would die for you have to wonder why you're alive.'

Bridge Company was located on the west side of the 2ID area, south of the Imjin River. Just its name connoted boredom. What did Bridge Company do when there were no bridges to be built, which was never. They had done a great job building the AIF. Amazing how fast it went in. LT Schikevitz remembered 'approving' its design almost on the first day of his new assignment as Assistant S3. No. His shop had nothing to do with it. This was a pure 8th Army concoction. It presented such formidable simplicity as-is, it was quickly approved and embraced. The construction commenced, three different segments, each under the command of A, C and Bridge Company of the 2nd Combat Engineer Battalion. The key feature was a standard 8-inch diameter steel pipe set in a concrete filled hole 3 feet deep, rising 8 feet above ground level to give vertical support to standard 8-foot wide chain link fence welded to these posts. This was topped by two metal struts welded to the sides of the pipe and thrusting upward in a V shape to which three strands of standard concertina wire was welded. Installing much of the 18 miles of Fence and fortifications in a matter of months, without mishap, across the American sector of the DMZ, was a great success. However, its completion became Bridge Company's dilemma.

With AIF maintenance assigned to others, it was now months since they had anything to do. Normally, nothing to do is bad enough on morale, but the finished Fence made it even worse. Before the Fence, North Korean Infiltrators passed through the Line nearly at will, any one of them possibly the guy who would shoot you dead. With the Fence in the way, the threat of infiltrators had flatlined, along with Bridge Company's vigilance. Nothing to do and no great concern for security whipped a flame of indifference that reached new heights when Dan handed the Bridge Company Commander, 1LT Michael Epperson his envelop. Oh, how Epperson's first words bellowed in the most declarative terms, "Nothing has happened at Bridge Company for so long, being told to do anything EVER AGAIN really pisses me off!"

Epperson continued. "Okay! So here you are with an envelope. Since doing nothing has worked out so well so far, tell Colonel Miller to take his envelope and shove it! We aren't doing' jack shit!"

Daniel listened to Epperson's entire rant attentively and as quickly as courtesy would allow, he departed with no response to his passionate decrees. He knew Epperson was a solid normal sort from a lower end family offering little prospects but two-year college. The Gulf of Tonkin incident changed all that. This naval engagement with the North Vietnam gunboats that never happened was made reason for a massive military buildup that followed. It also gave Michael a shot at Officer Candidate School. Epperson was in the moment. He could follow what was going on for what it was - a good guy, but not long on abstractions like, tomorrow might not be somewhat like today.

Daniel knew Epperson's inclination was born out of his bravado in front of his troops. Oh, how committed he was to protect them from doing anything. A class behind Dan at Belvoir OCS, Daniel knew that despite all his bluster, Epperson would do all in his power to rouse the troops, load up the trucks with prescribed gear and head out to their designated field location to set up camp with a defensive perimeter. However, Daniel winced at what this was going to look like. Bridge Company had been on break way too long.

The next stop was C-Company, again south of the River, on the eastern side of the 18 mile DMZ manned by the 2ID. Daniel did not know much about C-Company but did know they were busy enough that their morale would most likely not be as-in-the-toilet as Bridge Company. Daniel also knew the C-Company Commander a bit, eating dinner with 1st LT. Dave Fiescher at officer's mess for several months before he was shipped out of 2nd Combat Engineer Battalion HQ to be C-Company Commander.

Daniel universally held ANY West Pointer in high esteem, knowing that during their 4 years of training, they endured many times over the rigor of OCS. Daniel found OCS grads just fine for the same reason. He knew they had all made the cut physically and mentally. Fiescher was a ROTC officer. Daniel held all ROTC officers suspect until proven otherwise, since they had not survived the rigors of OCS or the Point. Fiescher was no exception.

In many ways he was up to the mark, but some of his attitudes seemed underlaid with an unearned overblown sense of entitlement. As the youngest of four siblings in an upper middleclass family, he was doted on by both parents and three sisters. Despite his short stature, endomorphic body, mediocre face, average wit and lack of grace, Fiescher saw himself as a special person and the rest of the world better get used to it. Daniel had seen lots of guys like him in OCS. They either had their sense of entitlement adequately pounded out of them (outwardly at least) or they washed out. For Daniel, Fiescher was evidence that ROTC presented no such filters. Further. Daniel and others found Fiescher squirmy, with a broad range of subtle gestures and body language, succeeding or failing to manipulate the reality around him to match his self-proclaimed importance.

All in all, Daniel found himself a bit shocked, uncomfortable, but not surprised by his outburst to the envelope when he shouted into Dan's face, "Tell the Colonel 'Fuck this shit! What are we supposed to do? Go out in the field in the dead of winter, below zero for God's sake! And then we camp out in the middle of nowhere. And then the war starts. Then they start overrunning us. Then the nukes come. Hell man! We can die just as nice RIGHT HERE. Where it's warm. And the food is good, and we sleep in our bunks, not out there doing bullshit. Tell the Colonel I'm not doin' shit, staying right here and tell the Colonel he can kiss my ass."

At this Daniel did respond, probing to see how serious Fiescher was, a bit over the top even for the 2nd Infantry Division's bad morale. It was nothing happening since 1953 putting everyone in a state of such high lollygag, just fooling around, mocking procedures for too long. Regardless of how low the morale, this was the kind of stunt Fiescher would pull and Daniel knew it. After a bit of cajoling, Fiescher calmed down, modulated his speech a bit and drifted off to a blank far-away stare upon which Daniel took his leave, satisfied with Fiescher's nearly imperceptible nod as an adequate good-bye.

On the way to A-Company, crossing Freedom Bridge over the Imjin River into the DMZ, Daniel mulled over Fiescher's latest antics. The rant offered no clues but the more he thought about his blank stare, the more convinced Daniel became it was the look of someone who had been feigning superiority for a lifetime and now had to prove it to himself and others that he was who he insisted he was. Daniel speculated that it would be a C+ all around, matching what he thought of Fiescher. Time would tell, and that was coming fast.

And now came the part Daniel had looked forward to—seeing his 'ol bunkmate' at Battalion, Bill Phiefer III. Just the way Bill stood there, so self-confident, not in a boastful way, but in all his moves, so free of doubt around the edges that you were drawn to him just to see if some of his confidence would rub off on you. Bill had an A-list face, but with no distinctive features like a Redford that made him stand out. The face was pleasant to behold and offered an easy peephole into his soul, quite an expanse of knowledge and calm expected of a Harvard grad. Since Bill was easy with his privacy, spending time with him revealed layer after layer of secrets and mysteries of his amazing self-confidence.

There was one rule. Bill made it clear within minutes of first acquaintance that there was one thing about him that was not going to rub off on you—money beyond your comprehension and his. Other than that, Bill was always ready with a genuinely friendly, 'What's your name?'

Bill Pheifer was of the Boston Phiefers, with wealth constantly bubbling up from rents and royalties from ventures initiated before the Revolution. Bill spent his year between prep school and Harvard on a 10-month grand tour of Europe escorting his grandmother, enjoying the excesses reserved only for his crowd. Daniel figured something happened on that world trip, way out of the comfort zone of Commonwealth Avenue, that morphed this super rich-guy-from-Boston into an interested citizen of the World.

Daniel saw Bill as a kind of Marcus Aurelius, stoic, non-flashy yet so superior you wondered if he could have a friend his equal. Like an FDR knock-off, Bill saw everyone else as the base of his own power. Whatever Bill could do to empower others empowered him. Right now, that meant taking a commission rather than weaseling his way out of it like the rest of his demographic. Bill's solid like-a-rock approach to life, his style and boundless patience was a value-add to all who served with him. Daniel thought Bill's expecting and receiving trust across such a huge social divide increased trust throughout the ranks. There was Bill doing just what he set out to do, improving the world starting with whoever was next to him at the time.

     Unremembered Victory

Somehow not surprisingly, Bill put in for A-Company Commander. A-Company meant you lived north of the Imjin, below the Fence, in the DMZ. It was by far the most dangerous assignment of all. You were in harm's way day and night by every North Korean agent that had snuck through the Fence the night before. No one was selected for A-Company. Once the position opened, the Colonel gave it to the first to volunteer. This time that volunteer was Bill.

Best thing about the draft, everyone meets everyone else, and because of Bill, Daniel felt more complete. Oh, and what did Daniel think of Bill's decision to take on A-Company? Noblesse obliges. Period. To borrow a line from Nabokov's novel Pale Fire, 'his honor had perfect pitch'.

Daniel knocked on the door to Bill's billet, or bedroom. Bill was lying on his bunk in a nondescript mood. He received the envelope and dismissed it casually. "Yeah" Bill mumbled in a throw-away tone, "We've been getting ready for this since the Line lit up with The Pueblo seizure two days ago. Let me see those coordinates and we are out of here."

Then, like an afterthought, Bill asked Daniel, "Hey, stick around and watch what's next." Bill was literally beginning to glow over the prospects of what was about to happen. The orderly room began to fill with platoon leaders and senior Sergeants with no one smiling, and the sounds were muffled with nervous coughs and faint whispers. One of the Sergeants gathered the nerve to ask the question, "LT. Pheipher, I understand that there are mass movement of troops across from our sector and trucks bringing in more North Korean soldiers, can you verify?" Bill looked at the gathering and boomed out, "It's true, the shit may be hitting the fan." Dan knew then that this was damned serious because Bill never used foul language and consistently discouraged it.

"Gentlemen", LT. Pheipher began reading from a dispatch, "At 02:30 PM the day before yesterday, the USS Pueblo, a non-combatant Marine Research vessel, after taking lethal fire that killed one crewman, its entire crew was seized on the high seas by North Korean gunboats and is now being held in in Wonsan Harbor." Bill went on to say, "Large North Korean troop movements have been detected which intel says could be anything from a runup to a South Korean Invasion to a response to our possible reprisals against North Korea for seizing the Pueblo. We are on High Alert. That means a war could start any time. Our orders are to stand and hold. You understand what that means."

"Every swinging dick in A-Company, until further notice, is no longer a combat engineer. Every one of you are Infantry soldier as of right now. That includes clerks, mechanics, medics and cooks...the whole bunch of you. Everyone must wear full combat gear always, each man with their rifle at the ready, with five magazines of ammo and four grenades. Tonight, we bivouac along a stretch of the AIF and remain there as long as the alert lasts. Every vehicle must be sandbagged in the floorboards, windshields down and all canvas tops removed. Most of you have faced the fire already. It looks like there is just going to be a whole lot more of it. We move out at 1700 hours. Good luck everyone."

How did it turn out? As expected, A Company performance was stellar. Both Bridge and C Company eventually did get in position, but along the way discovered half their trucks would not run, and half of their ammunition was too old to shoot. Normally all this would have been laughed off, forgotten in a rapid return to high lollygag. That was the old normal. The new normal was being forged by 2 Star 2nd Infantry Division Commanding General Izenour in his first Command Briefing since he was chewed out by General Bonesteel. While LT. Schikevitz was mounting up with his three envelopes, the 2nd Infantry Division senior staff was hunkered down waiting to hear their fate from their Commanding Officer.

WHITE ROOM
Cream

In a white room with black curtains
Near the stations black roof country
No gold pavements-tired starlings
Silver horses ran down moonbeams
In your dark eyes dawn-light smiled
On you leaving my contentment
I'll wait in this place where the sun never shines
Wait in this place were the shadows run from themselves

     Unremembered Victory

6

ALL THAT IS WRONG IS NOT DUE TO THOSE WHO CAUSE IT BUT TO THOSE WHO LET THEM

The 2ID Command HQ Board Room was abuzz with speculation, this being the morning after the Brigade Commander was relieved. There was a low-grade general mayhem among the attendees prior to General Izenour entering the room. No one could stop talking about the Colonel being so unceremoniously relieved of command and ordered to leave the country just 16 hours earlier, all that for just 2 GIs asleep on duty. Word had it that the relieved Colonel was so humiliated he had his Jeep driver take him directly to Kimpo, Korea's international airport. He did not go by his billet to collect his gear. He left with what he was wearing on the next military aircraft leaving Seoul not landing in Korea. It seemed like each senior officer in the room was finishing the sentence of the other, telling Izenour stories starting with the two Brigadier Generals (1 Star), both looking apprehensive and scared, talking to each other.

Brigadier General 1 said to Brigadier General 2, "I'm next. No question. Though he has barely shown his face much, scuttlebutt is he knows I have been just as inattentive and dismissive of this mission as anyone. We all have. Fifteen years is a long time for nothing to happen. I really screwed up by not shaking this tree the first day I got here. But what to do when the guy in charge seems so much more detached than you are."

Brigadier General 2 said, "No. I can assure you that I am next to go, having more time in grade than you makes me more senior. Only humiliating the highest-ranking officer will have maximum effect on the chain of command. Do we even know this guy? He gets here a half year ago and except for the weekly briefings and uneventful polite dinners … who is he?"

Brigadier General 1 speculated, "Well, I would say someone who relieved a Bird Colonel on the spot is no longer detached. But who was to know? Hell. Everybody knows that ever since he got here, he spent more time on the parade field at the 2ID Flagpole (jargon 2ID Headquarters), than anywhere else. I can hardly remember him even going off base. Most of the Company grade officers have heard of him, never met him."

The other Brigadier General added, "Oh! The parade field. I watched that epic unfold. Many think of it as the 2nd Civil War, this time the Union Army was the predominately African American honor guard soldiers. What a war that is. Izenour, the tall Texan, lectures. He demands. He cajoles. He threatens. He screams, and when the music starts to play, the honor guard does it their way just like before."

The first Brigadier General pontificated, "Give him a break. You and me both, and nearly all in this room—- It's the boredom. Nothing happens. I guess trying to get the parade right gave him a sense of purpose when everything else about the mission seemed to have no meaning at all. We sure have meaning now!"

Brigadier General 2 said ironically, "But the guy talks to no one. Have you had a real conversation with him? And he is our direct boss."

Brigadier General 1 said, "I was two years behind him at West Point and he did not talk to anyone there either, but not from others not wanting to be his buddy. That he was in the bottom third of his class does not help, but then every West Pointer in this room, on the entire DMZ, as we all well know, are in the bottom third of their class. I think it funny we are like where they send the Bad News Bears, out of the public eye where, if we screw up, no one will ever know."

Brigadier General 2 grimaced, "Well, get ready to be busted! He's coming through the door!"

There is general bustling in the room. The 2-Star Major General Frank M. Izenour stood before his two 1-Star generals, some dozen Colonels behind them, among other ranking officers in the room. As the General hit the podium, all came to their feet and offered the best salute they had. Shoulders back, you bet, but when General Izenour did not return their salutes after many seconds of high brace, their arms sheepishly cascaded down, one following another, to their sides.

General Izenour began in a powerful commanding voice, "Gentlemen. I got my ass kicked yesterday by General Bonesteel for damn near dereliction of duty. I, like you, fucking deserved it for letting procedures become so lax that 31 North Korea commandos casually waltzed through our

                                                    Unremembered Victory

ranks, down to Seoul and came close to killing the South Korean president and our Ambassador.

"We are not going to look back. You are all under orders to only look forward and come up to speed fast enough that we pose enough of a deterrent to invasion that Joe does not even try. Meanwhile, be informed that we are in a news blackout. These are grim times. The huge battle for Wey in Vietnam isn't going well while the whole Vietnam Theater looks like it's coming apart. So, it's our job to make sure there is only one-Vietnam. Just so you will know how serious things are, President Johnson just called up the Reserves for the first time since the Korean War, 11,000 Navy and Air Force personnel to get a nuke strike ready. Reports are that all twelve Atomic Cannons and some dozens of portable two-men carry nuclear devises are at the ready."

Izenour then looked around and saw what he hoped he would see, a group of men ready for a fight, one that had to be won or NOBODY went home. He continued, "Now what about us. We tracked down the two GIs who let the commandos through. They are not bad people. They are just fucking piss poor shit soldiers. Yes! I relieved the Brigade Commander over nearly half the men on the Line for just two GIs asleep at their post because I have exactly no time at all to make this pile of shit into something that will, like I said, give pause to 380,000 armed North Korean soldiers massed above us. May I remind you; we are facing the 4th largest Army in the world ready to jump. Intelligence's take is they are testing our resolve to resist a full-on invasion. RESOLVE! I will show you RESOLVE, shoving it up your butt so hard it can only come out of your mouths as fucking HARD ORDERS. I need screaming up and down this Line all the time about anything at all out of line, and there is no shortage of that. I want nothing but hard orders all day and all night until we are an Army. Just be consistent. In the days ahead, you can depend on me to keep showing you what consistent IS.

"Gentlemen. We have something else in our favor. It is worse than you may have heard. To make Vietnam quotas, the Department of Defense, ostensibly as part of President Johnson's War on Poverty, in the name of increased opportunity for the poor, have been inducting the totally unqualified and giving them a ticket only to Vietnam. Men unfit for service have been sucked out of the hills, the ghettos, the prisons and mental health system. It's called 'The 100,000 Program', named after the number of mentally and morally unqualified soldiers sent to Nam each year to make quota without touching the college students and Reservists. I am telling you this because it is no small thing that none of that crap is on our shores. We are assigned ONLY ORDINARY soldiers that passed all induction tests. No one from the bottom and no one from the top, including me. I say, give us 4,000 ordinary Americans like what we have right here, right now, in times like these, and we can push back the sea. That is about what it's going to take. Do not take it lightly that you CAN ENTER SCREAMING with impunity. So JUST DO HARD ORDERS, because you can, when you need to, which, as I said, right now, is all the time, until the whole thing is right and stays that way."

One of the Brigade Commanders who could not withhold his curiosity about the news blackout, hesitantly asks, "Sir, I talked to my wife last night. She said it is true. There has been ample mention of The Pueblo Incident and the Blue House Raid but none in the papers yet about the casualties we are taking on the Line. Why is this, sir? I would like to have something to tell the men."

General Izenour gathered his thoughts, changing demeaner he calmly responded, "Even your lowest security clearance guys can hear this. This is just my speculation. If the Line holding is not news, then the Line folding is also not news, so going nuke can proceed without the muss and fuss of public opinion. As I said, just speculation."

"Despite everything, I commend every one of you for getting us this far with the one thing that matters most: TRUST among our Korean hosts we are here to protect. No small task, gaining and holding this good ground we stand on right now to face the fire in front of us, and due to your leadership to date, will not have to worry about fire from behind. Now get out there, kick ass, don't let up. Get the men more fucking afraid of your wrath than enemy bullets and we have a chance."

General Izenour then barked in a commanding sharp voice, "DISMISSED!"

JUMPIN' JACK FLASH
The Rolling Stones

I was born in a crossfire hurricane
And I howled at the morning driving rain
But it's all right now, in fact, it's a gas
But it's all right. I'm Jumpin' Jack Flash …

7

JANIS JOPLIN
"I CAME FROM NOT MUCH. LOOK AT ME NOW.
I AM BIG. I AM HUGE. I AM POWER.
IF I AM THIS BIG, HOW BIG ARE YOU?"

The next day, Dan was standing on the side of Barrier Road just south of the AIF waiting for his Jeep driver to pick him up to inspect a fortification under construction that he designed. Two days after the Pueblo was seized on the high seas, this was the third day of sporadic sounds of gun fire and grenade concussions up and down the Line 24/7.

But for Daniel, he was not always this close to the action. When fresh from Ft. Belvoir Combat Engineer OCS in April of '67, he spent his first two weeks in country at a University in Seoul attending 'Cold War School' where, like every other in-coming officer, he was sensitized to Korean culture by being taught about all aspect of their history, religion, economy and social order and aspirations. Daniel then reported to his assignment at Camp Peterson as Headquarters Company Executive Officers of the 2nd Combat Engineer Battalion. Located safely some five miles south of the Imjin River, the southern boundary of the DMZ, Dan had no mission in the organization but to keep the mess hall running, the lights on and the area swept. The only time he did anything that remotely resembled action was the 'ammo detail'.

His job was to drive a whole truck full of ammo too old to use anymore to a depot for its disposal. Only 'in country' a month, Dan had become well acquainted with a Korean underclass that populated the villages and towns of the DMZ as well as the rest of Korea. Referred to as 'slicky boys', they fulfilled the role of pimp, bookie, fence, fixer and thief, all under the radar. Legend had it that in Seoul there was a 'Beggar King' who, in mass ceremonies, married the aging prostitutes with the aging thieves to assure the posterity of their guild. As their epithet implies, their one vocation of grave concern to the Army was stealing.

So, Dan, entrusted with so little, was dead-on determined to deliver all the ammo without any of it becoming Korean motif (quite compelling) souvenir ash trays, wall plaques and cocktail table knick knacks sold in

                                                                      Unremembered Victory

the villages AND the PXs. Not a small task given that the only route to the depot was through Yonjego, 'Slicky Boy Central'. In exchange for looking a bit foolish, from the time his truck entered Yonjego, loaded to the brim with old ammo, to when it was back to rural areas, Dan hung spread eagle out the door of the truck holding onto the roof with one hand and brandishing his standard issue 45 Pistol in the other, with a look on his face that said, "Yes, the safety is off!"

Across the board, however, Dan as Headquarters Company Executive Officer was there, but just taking up space. Perhaps it was entirely in Daniel's head, but he got the feeling that if Jewish, you were not even doing that. You did not have to look far to see where such sentiments came from. Whenever Dan asked his uncles who were at Normandy and the Bulge what it was like to be fighting the Germans to liberate the Jews, they all told him they were far too busy getting ready to fend off the next anti-Semitic blindside remark or gesture from their fellow soldiers to give much thought to that.

It was not that far off, just 25 years before, and Daniel's generation very much had been handed a hall pass. Daniel could count on just two hands all the times it was his turn to face a taunt since he was born, and in the Army not even ONCE, overtly. Thank you, USA. However, under the covers, Dan continued to feel invisible among the other officers.

Then on a steamy hot June night, the first reports of the Israel-Arab Six Day War came in. At first there was broad speculation whether it was just an incident or a real military operation. On the second night, it started. The two Battalion XOs, and 2nd Division Liaison Officer, kind of Battalion's management team, sans the Colonel, went out back behind the Officer's Club to shoot skeet as they often did after dinner. But that night their voices got louder and louder over how this is just plain bullshit. We all know its bullshit and when they figure what's really going on, it will be bullshit!

On the third night, their proclamations were more slurred, yelled into the night at no one in particular, but Daniel thought they wanted him to hear, which he did. There were drunken sincere outbursts like,

"It's their OWN GROUND. They've had 20 years to get ready. Their intel network must be so complete. IT'S THEIR OWN GROUND!"

On the fourth night it was much worse. It started early and got louder with occasional discharge of shotguns, allegedly at skeet. Before very long, Daniel noticed Sergeant Oliver, S3 Staff Sergeant, standing at ease near the skeet shooters with a loaded M14 by his side. When asked what brought him up to Officer's Hill, he said he was told to stand close to make sure this debating club did not hurt each other or anyone else.

OH! Did they yell that night, screaming like maniacs, desperately holding on to the beliefs about Jews they rode in on? That Jews are not like other people having gone to ovens without a struggle. Where is evidence of their courage, of their honor to die the way they did? What's to be trusted in combat?

The fifth night (there was no sixth night) was surprisingly quiet. They did not shoot skeet at all and sat sullenly around the officer's club, working hard not talking about anything that had anything to do with the soon to be called Six Day War. First thing the following Monday morning, Daniel's HQ Company Commanding Officer told him to report to the Battalion Commanding Officer. When he entered the room, there was the Colonel, Dan's soon-to-be-boss Captain McDowell, S3 Operations Officer, and all the regular skeet shooters. Daniel was told he was reassigned as Assistant S3 Operations Officer. His new duties were any field assignment that tapped his skills as a graduate Civil Engineer and/or put him in the most danger possible.

Everyone was smiling, the mood was very upbeat, Daniel was delighted to have something real to do and they all seemed hot for the 'experiment to begin'. When Daniel was dismissed, he saw it. It seemed a friendly respectful gesture he would see again in tough spots. It was a subtle waste height hand movement pretending to throw sand at his feet so that he was metaphorically standing in the desert. Then, like any Israeli, Dan could do ANYTHING. In the months to come, Dan felt like a science fair project watched by everyone to see how it would turn out. One thing was certain, LT. Daniel Schikevitz was no longer invisible, especially when he showed up for dinner each night still in one piece. As for Daniel, raised much more Southern than Jewish, none of this mattered all that much.

What did matter was getting a round off if he took the hit out there. The warm gun in his hand would tell the rest.

As mentioned, Dan's assignment started in June '67, a long way back before January '68, with Daniel waiting for his Jeep driver on the side of the AIF Barrier road mentioned at the beginning of this chapter. Little had happened in between. Occasional skirmishes left 12 GIs Killed in Action (KIA) that year, with three times that many wounded, several due to friendly fire accidents. The action was spread out over a lot of time, so it felt like not much was going on. Now it was January 26, the third day of bang bang everywhere all the time.

Get ready. Dan was about to become part of something most rare, 'The Army of the Republic'. His rights-of-passage to this holy ground started when Dan first noticed a Jeep approaching and belatedly saw a full Bird Colonel (rank insignia is an eagle with its wings spread) glaring back at him. It was only when they made eye contact that Daniel thought to himself, 'Hey! Perhaps I should solute this guy.' Bringing up his hand caused his body to shift and the dirt shoulder at the edge of a drainage ditch behind him gave way, causing him to stumble backward slightly as he completed the salute.

Instantly he heard the screeching of Jeep tires on the dirt road. A great cloud of dust was kicked up into the air by the violence of the skidding. Out of this swirling cloud of beige air emerged a tall, forty something Bird Colonel advancing toward the hapless Lieutenant with a storm of words pouring out of his tortured mouth that went something like …

> "We've got shit to pay out here and you are clearly part of the shit. You are the sorriest officer I have ever seen. It's one hell of a shame that this is all we have out here. This must change. This can no longer be. You need to take your sorry ass and make it over into something that remotely looks and acts like an officer. We are doomed if this shit does not stop. DO YOU HEAR ME! Get your shit together. That's an order! Be what you've got to be out here, not the shit bird you are now."

Just as suddenly as it began, it ended. The Bird was back in his Jeep and drove away. Dan's Jeep driver got to see the whole thing play out silently on Daniel's face, including Daniel's Ah Ha! moment. Dan had heard that General Izenour's rant had been a doozy just yesterday morning and the brass scattered like roaches after it was over. That Bird had too much rank to not have been at the briefing. Daniel said to his Jeep driver, "That was not a reprimand. You don't get dragged to the gates of hell for a bad salute. That was 'TRAINING'! Take me to the surveyor site. Maybe screaming will fix what until now has been unfixable."

So off they drove, along the Barrier Road just south of the Anti-infiltration Fence, passing one gate after another that led to combat roads north to each guard post. Their Jeep was waived through a gate onto a rough combat road that cut through hills and then mountains to far off Guard Post Charlie. Driving slowly, they came upon the seven-man surveying crew assigned to LT. Schikevitz, four GIs and 3 KATUSAs to survey and record the alignments of the new Barrier Road and the roads to each Guard Post. In these pre-GPS times, that meant using transits, plumb bobs and measuring tapes (chains) to set survey control points (hubs in the ground) where one centerline crossed another, projected down the next straight stretch of road. They were repeating this task from the gate to the guard post. Daniel's Jeep coasted to a stop. All Daniel could think of was the ass chewing he just got and now that a war was on, no more Mr. Nice Guy, as he walked toward the working men screaming …

> "WTF is going on here. This whole site is lollygagging bullshit. Where's your flak jackets, your helmet, your weapons, and PRAY tell, may I ask the ULTIMATE QUESTION, where is your ammunition. You don't have to tell me. I will tell YOU. It's all back in the truck, except you are not really sure where the ammo is."

Sam, the 3 stripers in charge of the survey team interjected, "But sir, our helmets will throw the compass bearing off … "

Sam had a great personality. That was a problem. Everyone liked each other way too much. Daniel responded screaming even louder,

> "Azimuth my ass! You are shooting points and turning angles and your helmet will not get in the way of anything but keeping a bullet from putting the inside of your head on the outside of your head. Here are the rules. Joe (the North Koreans) is on constant lookout

for easy bullshit bozos like you. When he kills you all, you will have it easy. YOU WILL BE DEAD! I will still be alive having to live with this shit for the rest of my life and I am just not going to do it. I will be back, and you will be STRAC!" (**St**rictly **Ac**cording to regulations).

Daniel entered screaming and left screaming, mounting his Jeep and driving away, returning salutes over his shoulder. For the next few months, entering screaming became Daniel's favorite thing, and but for one GI who flipped a Jeep joy riding, breaking his collar bone, everyone under his command got home without a scratch.

THE BALLAD OF BONNIE AND CLYDE
Georgie Fame

Bonnie and Clyde were pretty lookin' people
But I can tell you people They were the devil's children,
Bonnie and Clyde began their evil doin'
One lazy afternoon down Savannah way,
They robbed a store, and high-tailed outa that town
Got clean away in a stolen car,
And waited till the heat died down,
Bonnie and Clyde got to be public enemy number one
Running and hiding from ev'ry American lawman's gun.
They used to laugh about dyin',
But deep inside 'em they knew
That pretty soon they'd be lyin'
Beneath the ground together
Pushing up daisies to welcome the sun

8

… THIS GOVERNMENT, THE WORLD'S BEST HOPE …
THE ONLY ONE WHERE EVERY MAN WOULD MEET INVASION
OF THE PUBLIC ORDER AS HIS OWN PERSONAL CONCERN
[JEFFERSON'S 1ST INAUGURAL]

Two weeks later, it was a dark cold night in Kimpo Airport outside of Seoul with visibility of less than 200 feet. Cyrus Vance—US Secretary of State, and two assistants, were at a distance getting off a big airplane at Kimpo Airport. They were met by 4 Star General Bonesteel—8th Army Commander and James Porter, US Ambassador to Korea. Everyone shook hands, followed by the usual greeting gestures. As you get closer you can see them gathered around a small bubble top helicopter ready to whisk them in a quick run to HQ in downtown Seoul."

Ambassador Porter said, "I regret this ancient little helicopter is all we could swing today. There are only six Huey's in the country and they're all out, eyes-in-the sky, looking for a possible follow-up 2nd commando follow-up to the Blue House Raid. Boy those North Korean commandos were good. Scary as hell they have guys that good. We are impressed with Washington too; you are getting here in just over two weeks to start figuring out what the hell to do with this mess."

Vance explained, "Like here, in Washington, this place is seen as a backwater with all the good stuff going to Nam. You know they sent me here to make sure we have no second Vietnam."

Bonesteel directed everyone's attention to a more immediate problem saying, "Looks like we are one seat short. Why don't you just squeeze in next to me. Besides, this ride is without windows and you will be a great wind break."

Bonesteel said, "You have your hands full. Worried enough that Joe will jump, we are just as worried that the South is SCREAMING to invade the North. Either way, it means a second front to Vietnam already way too far in the crapper, recovering from the Tet Offensive and Battle for Hue. Not to worry. Cyrus. I watched you on the news when you quelled the Newark Riots in '65."

                                                                 Unremembered Victory

Vance recollected, "True. But all I had to do was end what was really a police riot by getting the National Guard to put away their guns against a defenseless but fearless community. This mess of course is bigger in scale but in some ways the same."

As the chopper lifted off, Ambassador Porter yelled loudly, "We will have plenty of time to talk before the reception with Park and friends tonight."

Bonesteel said, "Meanwhile, I urge you to take a hard look down below at what may be the craziest mixture of bone crushing poverty and unbridled pride you will ever see anywhere. What a people. You'll see."

Once everyone arrived at 8th Army HQ, General Bonesteel brought Vance up to date with the latest developments and then everyone huddled around Cyrus Vance to hear what he had to say. Vance started off, "Thank you, General Bonesteel, great briefing. Pleased to see we are in lock step. Here are my marching orders from Washington. I will do all the talking tomorrow. We will entertain any position on their part as long as it does not call for a wider war."

Bonesteel warned, "Get ready Cyrus. They think this visit by you, the number 3 man in America, means just that. Worse. Park can't calm down over he and his family coming within a hairs breadth of being assassinated. He is obsessed that they are going to try again, making being on the offence his best defense."

Vance said, "Meanwhile, Charlie, glad to hear that all our nuclear cannons and atomic demolition munition units are on full alert as a message to Kim Il Sung to not even try. We are so beat up from the Tet Offensive that still has a lot of our armed forces in Vietnam pinned down. There is no way we can wage a second conventional war. Any bombardment of Seoul would have to be met by nukes to silence the North Korean guns."

Ambassador Porter piped in, "Easily said, but remember that treaty we all signed with Russia when Korea was broken into two countries in 1945 obligates Russia to defend North Korea as though it were its own ground. That makes a nuke used on North Korea is the same as a nuke used on Russia. Legally, the next explosion could legally be New York City."

Meanwhile, not far to the south, canvas was being taken off Nuclear Cannons. They are huge with a barrel that makes it look like any other cannon, just bigger. Weighing in with a 180 mm bore, that's 11 inches. There were at least 12 Atomic Cannons in Korea ready to shoot multiple atomic warheads into North Korea with a range of 7—10 miles to stop any bombardment by the North on the South. For the 2ID, orders are simple. Don't give up a foot of ground. Make the enemy mass on top of you. When enough are piled on, nuke everyone?"

Bonesteel added, "Now, whether Park tries to go North is up to you, Vance. Whether Joe tries to come South, per intelligence, is all about how much resolve there is out on the Line. That's up to me. I take credit for building that barrier fence that has slashed North Korea incursions. I also take credit for the humiliation of 31 crack commandos slipping through that same fence unreported."

Ambassador Porter said, "Talk on the street is that the Line has seen a lot of turnaround."

Bonesteel strongly spit out the following name, "Frank M. Izenour, 2nd Infantry Division Commanding General. He's the one! He's the one who did it. Boy did I give him a hard time. He did not like being chewed out for the crappy moral in his unit. I think he's still getting used to having a second asshole. We may have gotten lucky. The way he relieved a Brigade Commander on THE SAME DAY was just the right message. Seamless screaming at everyone about everything all the time, getting the 2ID to be a crack military unit. Izenour is Just the prick that was needed at the right time."

Ambassador Porter concluded, "On that cheery note, I suggest we get dressed for tonight's Embassy reception with Park and his inner circle as a run-up to talks first thing in morning."

FIXING A HOLE
John Lennon, Paul McCartney

I'm fixing a hole where the rain gets in
And stops my mind from wandering
Where it will go.

I'm filling the cracks that ran through the door
And kept my mind from wandering
Where it will go.

And it really doesn't matter
If I'm wrong, I'm right
Where I belong, I'm right
Where I belong.
See the people standing there
Who disagree and never win
And wonder why they don't get in my door.

9
TO DEMAND THE TRUTH, TO SETTLE FOR NOTHING LESS THAN THE TRUTH, IS LIKE MAKING LOVE TO EXISTENCE

In the US Embassy, all were in dress blues as they entered a very formal state dining room with President Park and two other Korean high dignitaries at the head table in front of five tables of eight South Korean Military brass with lots of medals each. Toasts were made. President Park, slightly slurring his words said, "To the United States of America and your most honorable and wise President Johnson who has called us all together."

Cyrus Vance toasted, "Long live the great and revered Korean People. Together we will be successful in this time of mutual tragedy."

President Park tipped his glass and toasted, "To the US Secretary of State, Cyrus Vance, the third most powerful person in America, sent here for our war to reunify North and South Korea as the only permanent remedy."

Vance was a bit irritated by this sentiment but remained silent. Once the toast was over and dinner served, everyone was milling about in the hall, drinking and getting less formal by the minute. All eyes were on President Park, while in the corner, Vance is asking Bonesteel, "Is Park drunk? I see he is socking it down. He is slurring his words. Looks like he got started before he got here."

Bonesteel said, "Deplorable. Hardly blame him though. Bad enough they tried to kill him, but every Korean knows that it would not have been over until his entire family was dead. Don't worry. There is a long tradition of alcohol bolstering their courage before battle. Don't let this hair-down moment mislead you. I wish their soldiers were our soldiers."

Dinner was over, and the Banquet Hall filled with Korean generals and Americans socializing. Buttonholing Ambassador Porter, a Korean General slurringly declared, "Americans great. So, glad you here. Must make war. Only thing to do. So, humiliating not being safe anywhere. Cannot go on like this."

   Unremembered Victory

Another Korean General lamented to the Ambassador, "It never stops. Submarines raid our coast. People die. Infiltrators everywhere sneaking around all over the country trying to get our people to revolt. NO chance of that. All Koreans want to be one country again. Make you want to drink. I insist, have another. Another Korean General, trapping General Bonesteel in a corner, drunkenly lamented, "You hurt. We hurt. We blood brothers."

The next morning started off at the American Embassy with the big showdown between Vance and President Park. At the same time, Daniel and his Jeep driver, Simpson, were leaving 2nd Combat Engineer HQ and heading north through a thriving town of shanties when around the bend, he spies the town's one prominent structure, the railway station.

Daniel said to Simpson, "This was once just one of many train stations along the Pusan to Paris railroad. Now it is the last one. WTF. Look at all those kids pouring off that train that just pulled in. There must be a hundred of them. High school kids 15—18. Amazing. Look how clean and starched their black and white uniforms are. Weird. They are tying white bandanas with slogans painted on each one around their heads. Maybe it's a festival. I don't see any teachers. I wonder if they are playing hooky." Dan drove off, on his way north to the DMZ to do an engineer recon north of the Imjin.

At the same time, just 30 miles to the south, Secretary of State Cyrus Vance, Ambassador Porter, General Bonesteel, President Park and the medal bedecked Korean generals were seated in the front of the hearing room. There were some twenty other Senior South Korean Officers mixed with press, American Army brass and a couple of US government types.

Vance started off the proceedings by saying, "We agree that the aggression by the north to subvert your people and topple your government must stop. The US will do all in its power to safeguard South Korea in exchange for two things. One, South Korea agrees to put aside all plans to invade North Korea. Two, South Korea agrees NOT to participate in any USA efforts to free the Pueblo crew. In exchange, the United States will double down on the security of your nation and expedite the end to all the strife that you have so valiantly endured. Do I have your promise? No invasion!"

President Park said, "You put me in an impossible position. Every day, the North gets stronger in weapons and training. Their commandos were nothing like anyone had seen before. We have no idea how many more they have like that. Everyone believes that ONLY reunification will permanently end this trouble by ending its perpetrators."

Back up north, about the same time that President Park started this rant, Daniel was eating in an open-air dining hall on the way to Freedom Bridge. He saw the students, as many girls as boys, marching in formation, every fourth step their arms swung up in the air and they belted out in unison 5, 6 and 7-word slogans, each one louder and more spirited than the one before. Curious Daniel asked the Korean cook, "What are they saying?"

The cook said, "I try to repeat in English. They say …

> "To attack Blue House is grave insult!
> "This disrespectful act must be revenged!
> "There must be war for reunification!
> "Only total war gets our honor back!
> "Mighty and great are The Korean People!"

Daniel mentioned to the cook, "We have a lot of kids in the street demonstrating to stop war. I was one of them. Same passion and commitment, but these kids want to start one." Daniel got back in his Jeep and continued on his way thinking to himself, "Why are they protesting here? Where are the chaperones?"

Meanwhile, back in Seoul, Cyrus Vance was at the podium saying, "As you know The Tet Offensive is a humiliating defeat. Worse, our people are in the streets everyday screaming at us to get out of Vietnam."

This short statement leads to the lights being turned down in the meeting room as a film started… The words TOP SECRE sprawled across the screen. The film showed canvas being taken off an arsenal of Nuclear cannons. The documentary film stated that Atomic Cannons are good because they make sure we can win limited wars. The voice-over said,

                                    Unremembered Victory

"These are nuclear cannons. They can fire a nuke up to ten miles. There are twelve in Korea. This crew will soon have everything in place but the order to shoot."

The lights went back up and Secretary Vance said, "America cannot handle a second conventional war in Asia. As you well know that leaves us no choice but to use nukes if this thing gets out of hand. A SECRET op order will soon be issued called 'Operation Freedom Drop' to provide all the details.

Vance continued, "One way for your nation to restore Korean honor is to honor the lives of everyone else on this planet by your restraint to avoid a nuclear exchange."

Whereupon President Park snapped back, "If we do not invade, I will have a rebellion here. That is not in America's interest, South Korea in turmoil, fighting among ourselves. One tiny provocation, JUST ONE SPARK is all that is needed for mass hysteria sweeping us up into going North, like it or not."

Meanwhile, back up north, Dan was coming around the bend in the road, looking down the final approach to Freedom Bridge. He spied the students no longer in formation, just running across the bridge, screaming. He wound up stuck behind the last dozen or so kids overrunning a solid cordon of half-tracks with mounted 50s amazingly able to get parked in time tread to tread across the entrance to the bridge. Though an impressive defense, impossible to get through or around, the students only saw it as something to scramble over. As one of the half-tracks moved out of the way to let Dan's Jeep through, Daniel screamed at the dumbfounded guard, "How could you let these kids get through?"

Just as loud the guard yelled back, "What to hell are we supposed to do, Sir? Shoot them? They ran right at us and when we tried to block their way, they just ran right over us, yelling and screaming, ignoring the guns and … "

In hot pursuit, Daniel did not wait to hear the rest. He caught up to the students about a half mile down the road where they were trying to climb the AIF just installed a couple of months before. Easily scaling the chain link lower part, they were having no success in getting through the triple strands of concertina wire welded on top. By the time Daniel got there, they were all flailing about in a frantic array of elbows and kneecaps, determined to squeeze through.

Daniel, now out of his Jeep, looked around and found himself promoted to officer-in-charge by simply being the only officer there. Just then some trucks started to arrive. Daniel knew this stretch of the AIF well. So close to Freedom Bridge, just one of two ways to cross the Imjin River, he had personally beefed up this stretch of fence with a triple tier minefield. Knowing this, Daniel screamed with all his might,

> **"DO NOT LET THEM GET OVER THE FENCE**! Get them off the Fence and into the trucks. Anyone of them clears the Fence, they will surely be blown to bits in the minefield.

By this time there were about 40 GIs, counting the truck drivers, working the crowd. With a bit of a ruckus, they dragged each one of the students off the AIF, walked them to a truck and helped them on board. The second no one was looking, the same students squirmed out of the truck and bolted back to the fence. By this time the KATUSAs had reported to Dan what they had overheard from the students. Their plan was to run helter-skelter into the DMZ, find North Korean Army soldiers, attack them with their bare hands and make them martyr them. They saw it a small price to pay for starting the war that must be fought to unify their country since there will never be peace until then. The more students that die, the surer there is war.

More trucks arrived just to get backed up, only adding to the confusion since they could not keep the kids in the trucks that were already there. Worse, with each attempt the students were figuring out new tricks for squirming through the concertina wire, getting over the AIF and dashing 60 feet before detonating the first mine, and with any luck, falling on a second one. That's how they were spaced.

Meanwhile, the Sea of Japan was choked with ships bristling with missiles, the atomic cannons rolling into firing positions. The Atomic Demolition Munition platoons in 8th Army were sleeping in uniform beside their hand-held nukes.

At the same time as the student DMZ riot started, back at the American Embassy, Vance was calmly stating to President Park, "Your passion for wanting to do what is best for Korea is quite understandable."

Raising his voice, a bit but not changing his engaging we-are-all-in-this-together tone, Vance went on to calmly say, "Unfortunately, this is not about just South Korea. The future of the whole world is in the balance. Here is what is wrong with going north. Seoul, as you well know, is within range of conventional North Korea artillery and rockets. With nearly 100% assurance, shelling of Seoul will start upon any invasion attempt by the South. If that happens, the US has no choice but a nuclear response because a conventional one is not an option due to being so bogged down in Vietnam. You have my complete assurance that America will not waver in our commitment to a common defense if North Korea were to come south, but in the name of international survival, I cannot offer the same if you go North."

President Park countered by saying, "I see your point, but I remain in a tough spot. So, what's in it for us if we do not go north?"

Meanwhile, back up in the DMZ, as student efforts to 'invade' North Korea raged on, a trick came to Daniel's mind to end this mess. Over the roar of people all around, Daniel shouted full throttle,

> "Throw them high in the air. Aim for students trying to get out!"

As soon as a truck had six or seven students on board, dazed or otherwise, Daniel barked,

> "MOVE! MOVE! Step on it! Go fast enough so they can't jump out!"

Everywhere two GIs grabbed a single student by their arms and legs, threw them high in the air so their bodies acted like big boxing gloves, knocking down students trying to get out. One truck after another took off like a shot, each delivering some half dozen or so students back to the civilian side of the bridge. As the students realized that their plan was not going to work, there emerged an Alpha Girl, their apparent leader, barking orders in Korean heard over the din that our KATUSAs translated on the fly …

"It no matter who kill you! GI just as good as North Korean! Strike them! Gouge their eyes out! Get them to kill you! If that no work, get their bayonet and kill yourself!"

The kids started grabbing the GIs with their bare hands, trying to gouge out their eyes. When that did not work, they started grabbing at their bayonets. They seemed to prefer African-Americans as though they may be more prone to violence. It did not work. As the swearing by the GIs grew louder, through it all, Daniel could be heard slowly repeating, "Steady. Steady."

The air was dense with swearing and screaming, yet not a single GI was close to losing it. Instead, they quickly developed a protocol for carefully and methodically grabbing student's harder, throwing them higher and driving the trucks away faster, with every move aimed at protecting life and ending violence. The thought of all those bruises and broken fingers and ribs from the rough handling made Dan smile. Those injures would heal without a trace but would remain their eternal internal badges of courage.

As the student ranks thinned, knowing it was all over, the Alpha Girl suddenly dropped to her knees, pushed a flat rock on the side of the road in front of her and then placed another flat stone on top of the first one. Then she reared her upper body back …

Thanks to Hollywood, Daniel knew exactly what the two rocks were all about. A popular movie just before Daniel's conscription was Robert Michener's Hawaii. The first half of the movie was about paradise lost, the King of Hawaii losing ground to persistent and manipulative intruders. Having lost all, alone on the beach, with the orchestra going full tilt, he puts a flat stone in front of him and then a second stone on top of the first, where upon he reels back and shoves his body forward so the front of his skull is bashed open like an egg. The Theater goes totally dark. INTERMISSION

Just as she was rocking back as far as she could, Daniel screamed a scream that could be heard all the way to Pusan…,

"GET THAT BITCH OFF THAT ROCK!!!"

Instantly four GIs had her by her hands and feet and she was airborne.

As the Alpha Girl was arching in the air, back in the American Embassy, Vance said, "Agree not to go North, and the US will double down on our military support starting with a Squadron of F16s fully loaded."

To this President Park blurted back, "NOW you have TRULY insulted me and my country!! In exchange for giving up our sovereignty over our own International affairs, America offers one squadron of F16s!"

Freeze frame of girl on her way down into the truck.

Vance looking Park dead in the eye and loudly countered,

"Two Squadrons!"

Now back at the riot site, freeze frame the Alpha Girl landing on the other students, stream video her final sprawling on top of two other students already in the truck, flailing about, with all color draining from her face as she feels the truck lurch forward, putting an end to her plans forever.

Back at the American Embassy, President Park declared, "DONE!"

MY GENERATION
The Who

People try to put us d-down (Talking' 'bout my generation)
Just because we get around (Talkin' 'bout my generation)
Things they do look awful c-c-cold (Talkin' 'bout my generation)
I hope I die before I get old (Talkin' 'bout my generation)

10

WITHOUT ENOUGH CARING
JUSTICE IS JUST THE STRONGEST WINNING EVERY TIME

Some weeks later, Daniel was checking up on the surveyors again, proceeding due west along Barrier Road alongside the south side of the AIF to where his survey crew was shooting points. As he approached, Daniel could see there was no improvement. They were all just as careless as ever.

Daniel said to his Jeep driver, Simpson, "Look at that. Same old shit. Looks like hard orders didn't do bubkis with these clowns, thinking it's funny mocking the rules and playing being bullshit. Pisses me off! Dan lamented to Simpson. Sam, you know Sam, their three stripers, despite this shit, is really a great guy. He showed me a picture of his wife once... what a babe! She looked like Dorothy Hamill, but more sincere. How could a guy with a wife like that be such a schmuck about his own life? Yelling louder is not going to do it. I think I need to try something more diplomatic."

Daniel dismounted the Jeep and walked toward the site SCREAMING louder than ever,

> "You know Sam, when Joe kills your fucking ass and all your men, I'm going to write your wife a letter and this is what it's going to say... 'Your husband is dead because he was a dumb fucking piece of shit who got himself killed, along with all his men, because he was a wise ass shithole who refused to take any measures to assure the safety of his men and himself ...'"

This time the result looked more promising as LT. Schikevitz drove away. Rather than the usual hollow 'We-will-try to-do-better-Sir' grin he got in the past, this time it was more that dark stare into space of someone whose core beliefs have just been ripped clear of their moorings.

All the way back home that night, as always, the Jeep endlessly bumped and lurched through the ubiquitous potholes and irregularities of the roadway. Throughout the Second Infantry Division there were no paved roads once you left Seoul, much less four lane highways. During the long stretches between rainstorms, vehicular traffic turned the surface to a half inch or so of pulverized dirt talcum powder. Every vehicle left a plume of dust behind it. As a result, the air along the more traveled stretches had a perpetual beige tinge.

Danial saw what he always saw as he passed through every large town to small village north of Seoul and south of the Imjin River — strings of little shops on both sides of a road surrounded by the ubiquitous timber and brown earth stucco walled and thatch roofed 'hooches'. There was always a woman or two perpetually tossing buckets of water in sweeping arcs onto the surface of the road in front of their shop to hold down the dust, while at the same time, in the dark interior others were sweeping dust out of their shops and houses. Daniel's mind wandered to one question that revisited him often. 'Why are these people so poor?'

He remembered learning in Cold War School that a central historic period of the Korean People was an uninterrupted 530-year run of Confucius rule under the Chosen Dynasty starting just before 1400 and not ending until just before the Japanese Takeover in 1910. Daniel wondered whether Confucian interest in material wealth was as we know it or something more cerebral that left no trace? He wondered enough to ask the librarian at Recreation Center 3, the one north of the Imjin, in the DMZ, to find him a book on Confucius economics. There it was, waiting for him just two days later. He popped it open and, and right on the first page, it read …

'A population which is numerically large, skilled, and with sufficient disposable income, provides a large market for the consumption of goods and services.'

Daniel read a bunch more and found it was a lot like Adam Smith's 'Wealth of Nations' (what not to like) stressing free will and conscious efforts to grow and nurture market as the best path to higher prosperity for all. Well, not exactly, but close. Some would argue exactly.

Backing up a step, Daniel had learned earlier that up until the Chosen Dynasty, Buddhism ruled the Peninsula starting about 100 BC. Early monks, finding teachings from foreign countries inconsistent with local traditions, developed a new holistic approach called Korean Buddhism.

It held the Peninsula together for 14 centuries. The number of Buddhist orders diversified and flourished, increasing the political power of the monks. However, this led to Buddhism's condemnation by the common people and marginalization by the aristocracy. The whole thing came crashing down with the rise of the Joseon Dynasty (1392-1908).

Central to this major regime change was the Joseon Dynasty sweeping Korean Buddhism aside and, as mentioned, replacing it with a Korean flavored Neo-Confucianism. Buddhism's most attractive here-and-now teachings celebrating actuality, were retained. The more arbitrary cosmic (like space opry) sagas were dismissed. So, 600 years ago, Neo-Confucianism came roaring out of the shoots full of high ideals and intent on progressive rule. The emperor's role was to empower people to improve themselves, holding true to Confucian belief that the people are the true power of the realm

Daniel remembered reading their list of accomplishments that made these rulers look like they all woke up every morning thinking only of what new ways the emperor could facilitate the people to be more prosperous. Such pursuits included universal education, ethics universities, agricultural almanacs, medical books, pharmaceutical catalogs and open court records.

The granddaddy of them all was good ol' King Sejong the Great, Dan's favorite. An early Chosen Dynasty Emperor, his attempts at Confucian Humanism are still celebrated today. It included all of the above, topped by something new, the 'Hall of Worthies', adding incentive for research in institutional traditions and social policy. Emperor Sejong left behind many quotes like …

> "The common people are the foundation of any country. It is only when this foundation is strong that a country can be stable and prosperous."

> "… amongst uneducated people there have been many who, having something that they wish to put into words, have been unable to express their feelings in writing …"

The latter statement explains why he created a Korean alphabet, Hangul. Desirous that all his subjects were able to learn to read and write,

King Sejong ordered the scholars of the Hall of Worthies to devise a simplistic alphabet that could be learned by an uneducated person in a matter of hours to days. Universal literacy enabled Confucius rule to be self-righting by recorded competent expression by a literate public as the one best bulwark against excesses of power.

So, while Emperor Sejong lived, and on and off thereafter, the whole Korean peninsula was able to be a Confucian state. For hundreds of years a competent, egalitarian, people-centric belief system became the basis for governance. It may have gone on, with higher levels of success, even until today IF Korea had not failed to repulse a Chinese Invasion in 1636. Ultimately, Korea became a client state of China starting in the 1840s as outcome of further military defeats. The Chosen Dynasty remained an independent country to manage their own affairs and they were not occupied by Chinese troops. On the other hand, all matters of international affairs were deferred to China. Interestingly, one reason for Korea's short comings in battle was their military class was smaller and held in far less esteem than the administrator class, in which leadership was measured almost entirely in scholarly achievement and demonstrations of fair mindedness.

Then it got worse. In 1894, China lost a war with Japan. This caused Korea, like a perk, to wind up a de factor client state of Japan. Fearing the worse, in 1896 the Emperor's wife, Mem, tried to recruit Western Powers to help protect their sovereignty against Japan since China could no longer do so. As a reward for her initiative, a small group of elite Japanese commandos came ashore at night, penetrated the palace, assassinated her, burned her body and threw her ashes to the wind by morning. Nothing was good after that. Japan spawned systemic corruption everywhere within the ruling elite. This led to eventual collapse of social institutions. Apparently, most of the accumulated wealth of that period went up in smoke or carted off when the Japanese took over 'administratively' in 1910. The only upside was that to exploit Korea's resources, Japan built a vast network of modern railroads to get the goods to the coast for shipment to Japan. All those railroad tracks and tunnels and bridges were left behind when Japan went home, leaving Korea with modern infrastructure for the first time. However, whatever

South Korean progress there was between 1945 and 1950 was swept away by the Korean War.

During the last six months of 1950, the entire nation, outside a 40-mile radius around Pusan (the Pusan Perimeter), were forcefully subjected to Communist rule. Daniel knew firsthand what that was all about, way beyond what he was taught in Cold War School.

While Dan was Headquarters XO, one of his duties was to oversee the bookkeeping of the mess hall and officers club. Before very long, Daniel and Mr. Chung Hu Yee, a Korean national, equivalent to the Battalion CPA, became good friends. Due to the nature of the work, Daniel and Chung were always in ear shot of each other. Over time they discovered they were kindred souls, curiosity junkies, never bored. Yee was a great storyteller and Daniel loved to hear good stories, so on many occasions Yee would tell Daniel 'again' all kinds of stories including why all South Koreans hated Communism with such a never-will-die passion. Mr. Yee said, In his own words …

"Wootenant Schawkawitz, war starts. I too young for Army so I am home when invading North Korean soldiers take over town. They don't stay long. They carefully select who to leave behind to run place after they move on. They look for town's biggest losers, both mean AND considered very good-for-nothing by all the rest. Biggest no-accounts among us now in charge. Only two North Korean soldiers remain to back up the new leadership with their weapons. Being the town bums, new leadership have no respect of the people. They must stay loyal to North Korean soldiers since all their power comes from them. Not only humiliating, but everyone constantly looking out to be casually hit hard on the side of your head just to show who boss or getting even for some long ago slight. All day we in fields, told what to do, no choices—- all agriculture belongs to collective. Night, that worst time. Every night—Communism School in school auditorium. Always the same. We no talk. Only they talk. Glories of socialism. Evils of capitalism."

Mr. Yee looked like he was back there, but now with a look of defiance he surely kept to himself at the time. He went on to explain, "Every night at meeting you were made to say things over and over, pound into our head hour after hour. Sit along all four walls facing the center, while

                                        Unremembered Victory

a once town lowlife, now leader, talks forever, standing next to North Korean Army guys. Couple other goons walk behind you. You start nodding off. BAM! No warning; clubbed on the side of head. BAM, someone else gets it, really hard. Night after night after night. Then American Army come. The town bums flee with North Korean soldiers. Now we hate Communism. Every Koran everywhere thinks same. Everyone KNOW Communism means night meetings, getting smacked in the head so hard head still ringing. For us that's Communism, forever, never change. Now we try to have democracy, but the elections are all fixed so that Chung Hee Park always wins. He was the head of the Army. Now head of us. He does many bad things but, overall Korea has lots of hope. One of our hopes is to have American democracy someday. It's easy to want but hard to get—one person, one vote. America lot like Confucianism but maybe even more not about king, not about state. Instead about each living person center of their own lives."

Daniel asked, "Mr. Kim. I have read about the Japanese take over in 1910. They came ashore and took over the government, army and navy, without firing a shot. I find that hard to take. Makes me think less of Korean people of the past. What happened. Is it true without firing a shot?"

Mr. Yee remained silent and stone faced, something he was good at when needed.

Daniel beseeched, "Was there any resistance?"

Mr. Yee said, "Well. You count suicides by some high Korean officials, shots were fired, but none at the Japanese. Please. I explain." Mr. Yee winced, reminded of this low point in the history of his country and grimaced, "Understand, Wootenant Shawikawitz. Not about our bravery. For quite a while we had been a protectorate of Japan after they beat the Chinese in war. Not hard to reduce us into being their colony. Careful mix. Subversion, coercion, and deception. Low point. We totally demoralized when they assassinated our Empress. They corrupt administrative class. reduce their authority over the people, culminating a terrible thing—the *Japan–Korea Treaty of 1907*. This Treaty so bad for Korea. Ended the Chosen Dynasty. Worse, allowed Japanese to supervise Korean affairs including putting their own people in high places in our government.

When the Japanese army came ashore to occupy country, it was just one more step to reduce us to being slaves. Then many resisted. All hopelessly suppressed and killed by army and police, now lead by the Japanese.

SAD EYED LADY OF THE LOWLANDS
Bob Dylan

With your mercury mouth in the missionary times,
And your eyes like smoke and your prayers like rhymes,
And your silver cross, and your voice like chimes, Oh,
Who do they think could bury you?
With your pockets well protected at last,
And your streetcar visions which you place on the grass,
And your flesh like silk, and your face like glass,
Who could they get to carry you?
Sad-eyed lady of the lowlands,
Where the sad-eyed prophet says that no man comes,
My warehouse eyes, my Arabian drums,
Should I put them by your gate,
Or, sad-eyed lady, should I wait.

11

ALWAYS STEP IN THE SAME PLACE TWICE
IF YOU'RE TRYING TO MAKE A TRAIL
NEVER STEP IN THE SAME PLACE TWICE
IF YOU'RE TRYING NOT TO LEAVE A TRACE

Daniel remembered not all that long ago when the casualties started to mount, everywhere it was the same. WTF. How to hell do we keep from getting killed? A big boost came when General Izenour pumped up the Imjin Scout Training Program, teaching best methods of patrol, ambush and warding off assaults on guard posts. Not all passed. The way the 2ID Command made a big deal over the latest graduates, everyone else could not help looking up to them. Once the regular ranks started looking up to the Imjin Scouts as a big deal, everyone started looking up to each other as a big deal just for being North of the Imjin River. Because Daniel was S3 Operations, he did Combat Engineer recon and project supervision all over the DMZ, from one end to the other. Daniel saw a seamless sense of belief in each other spread over all 4,000 GIs collecting hostile fire pay north of the Imjin, especially north of the Fence. With sound, steady leadership from Army and Division, the Line went to universal trust in one another, side-to-side and top-to-bottom, as the shortest path to carnal survival. Upon this proving to be a winning hand it quickly grew until EVERYONE North of the River became a bit of a part-angel priesthood of armed soldiers who, like Start Wars, completely believed in the mission and every man or woman next to them.

One of Dan's assignments right after the Pueblo was Seized and the DMZ War got going with a vengeance was to recon every road to every Guard Post and report on their condition and needed improvements. Boring enough but for one, Guard Post Gladys, for which there was no road at all. Starting at a gate at the AIF, GIs were forced to backpack in supplies up a near vertical hand over hand trail. Rapid reinforcement by motorized vehicle had not been possible since the Armistice in '53 when they froze the Line. Dan turned in the report and by the end of the week, Captain McDowell ordered Dan to engineer a road to GP Gladys pronto.

The very next day, Daniel and his Jeep driver, Billy Brune, who doubled as Engineer Tech Specialist, met up with the five-man Imjin Scout rifle team, three GIs and 2 KATUSAs assigned as security for their road flagging detail at the GP Gladys gate along the AIF. Siting the road would take some nine recons north of the AIF to flag the alignment to GP Gladys where no road existed before.

Their squad leader, SGT Tom Baker, saluted Daniel and Daniel returned the salute. It was a very good salute. Daniel was not expecting a salute that good, but for SGT Baker, it was his way of staying 'on the deal.' What was the deal? It was not about an individual soldier's performance being 'better' or 'worse' than others. Instead, SGT Baker found it a matter of just being in the moment, paying attention to everything as hard as you could, ready to do what had to be done, and if it had to be done, doing it as best he could. In exchange, if he got through this alive, he got to go home to the most amazing life ever. Why expect that? The recent past had been the 50s and early 60s when just about everywhere, even backwater Hattiesburg, Mississippi where he was born and raised, more money seemed be pouring up and down every street more every year. With his own two eyes, he had watched all kinds of people becoming middle class and beyond all around him. There was so much growth, promotions and prosperity, as the country rewarded everybody top to bottom for winning WWII.

Being on the Deal worked for LT. Schikevitz. North of the Fence, every next noncommissioned soldier he did not know walking toward him typically offered their record braking best salute of their entire life. As little as minutes later they might repeat this intrapersonal contest upon eye contact with another officer. Daniel had a friend who sat out his whole 2-year commission without ever leaving the Pentagon. He wrote Daniel that only an idiot would have themselves saluted in a combat zone, telling the enemy who to shoot first. Daniel wrote back that, "I feel a whole lot safer knowing the guys next to me thinks they are soldiers."

"Can you believe how this mangey bunch of conscripts is shaping up?" Daniel declared to Brune. Daniel was amazed how hardened and dependable some of the flakiest in the ranks were before The Pueblo Seizure. You know, I bet that's why I get those outrageous over the top solutes out there. They are not honoring me as a person, but as a symbol of the 2nd Infantry Division, those solutes are celebrations of the perceived goodness of the unit.

                                                    Unremembered Victory

About Tom, in 1966 he was picked up and swept along with some 960,000 other inductees that year. He knew it was coming since he had given up his student exemption status and was now 1A. There was never a question of heading to Canada to avoid the draft. A deep-seated loyalty Tom felt about his country pushed aside any thoughts of Canada and major personal doubts he had about the Vietnam War.

Some of Tom's friends thought him nuts while others lauded his decision. To Tom, it simply made sense, and more importantly, offered a way out of Hattiesburg. His next stop was Fort Benning, GA—Sand Hills Basic Training Center where he learned the necessary skills to survive in combat situations in Vietnam and a whole lot about life that would have never come his way.

In basic training, Tom's leadership skills were noticed. He was appointed as one of two leaders of the platoon. Tom was particularly pleased since the selection was made by all the platoon members with the blessing of the platoon Sergeant. The other guys were happy for him since he always seemed fair in assignments and had an uncanny ability to manage his time. For Tom, things came easy and he continually offered help to any guy unable to keep up with the situation. Upon graduation from basic training Tom was promoted to Private First Class. Again, the best part was none of his platoon members resented his promotion.

After finishing basic, Tom went on to Fort Leonard Wood, MO for advanced training in the effective use of various weapons, leadership, operational tactics, and map reading. Upon graduation eight weeks later, near the top of his class, Tom was promoted to Specialist 4th Class.

Tom remembered at the end of Basic, the entire battalion made formation in front of headquarters to receive assignments. As each name was called their destination was announced. The Republic of Vietnam was called repeatedly with an occasional Fort Meade, MD or Fort Belvoir, VA, but when Tom's name was called the officer called out "Republic of Korea." He turned to a soldier next to him and asked, "Did I hear right?" The soldier replied, "Republic of Korea is what he said, you're going from Little Korea to Big Korea." Fort Leonard Wood was known affectionately as Little Korea due to the similar weather and hills everywhere. That day, four other graduates had been selected for a Korean assignment as well and within the week Tom was in transit to the Republic of South Korea.

Now we flash forward, and here was Tom on a forested ridge in the DMZ north of the AIF on engineering recon security duty. Once a devastated battleground, the DMZ had by '68 lain somewhat frozen in time for the fifteen years since the end of the Korean War. As such, it had reverted to a natural wilderness almost entirely, making it one of the most pristine undeveloped areas in the world. It contained many ecosystems including forests, estuaries, and wetlands frequented by migratory birds. The zone served as a sanctuary for hundreds of bird species, among them the endangered white-naped and red-crowned cranes. This new wilderness was also home to dozens of land animals such as Asiatic black bears, lynxes, and other mammals. Pheasant and quail were constantly at your feet. And North Korean Infiltrators hidden everywhere.

Dan lead the flagging crew off the Jeep trail, taking a hard left up the ridgeline on foot, through undisturbed wilderness, much of full live oak climax. Daniel could not stop thinking how lucky he was to be out and about in this pristine natural wilderness, one of his favorite things, while on the clock, pulling hostile fire pay to boot.

It was on one of those sunny days, and on the lunch break, Tom asked Dan, "Sir, yesterday it looked like you had figured out how to get the road all the way to the top. How come you know how to do this stuff?"

Daniel smiled broadly and said, "You don't have to be all that smart or trained to figure it out. Just by insane coincidence, to try to avoid the draft, I worked seven months in the Los Angeles County Department of Public Works, Mountain Roads Division."

Tom interrupted and said, 'But you are a DC boy. How did you wind up out on the West Coast? Hell. You're still an East Coast kid."

"That is the most screwed up part. I was recruited by LA County Road Department on the East Coast as I was graduating with a Civil Engineering degree from the University of Maryland. They were recruiting from so far away because it was East Coast kids that were having the hardest time staying out of the draft. They figured that the hungriest graduates would jump at a critical works deferment that came with the Job. Count

　　　　　　　　　　　　　　　Unremembered Victory

me in. I drove to California, started up my job, but it did not work. My Bethesda Maryland Draft Board denied the deferment because, frankly my dear, they did not give two shits that I was critical to the success of the Feather River Project without which LA would have had to stop growing."

Tom, looking a bit wistful, suddenly blurted, "So that's how you know what to do. I watched. You did not look like you were guessing. There was no hesitation. You would walk some 50 feet higher from the last flag you placed and looking all around, then Bam! You would tie a ribbon on a tree branch or shrub nearest you and move on."

Daniel said with a smile, trying to keep it fun and not a lecture, "It's not rocket science. True, a lot of it I learned siting a road for the Castaic Dam Project, a right turn just as you start north up the Grapevine out of LA. The rest I learned in school."

Tom continued, "So, how do you do it? How do we get a road to Guard Post Gladys? It can't be easy. Every other Guard Post has a road to it for quick reinforcement when under assault. Makes sense that since Gladys, to this day, has no road, building one must be a bitch."

Dan took some pause to plan what he was about to say before he began, "Like everything else, I started off trying to figure out the easiest way up possible. It did not take long to rule out all the hillsides around the Guard Post, being on a promontory, the highest ground in the entire DMZ. They were all way too steep to even think it. A hike to the top told the tale. There was no road because, you are right, building one would not be easy. The only way up started over half a mile due east, at the far end of a half mile ridge, but even that was too steep until I could figure out its secrets."

Tom said, "Secrets, Sir? I don't mean to make fun of what you are saying, but hills don't have secrets."

Daniel, with a mock sneer, shot back, "No secrets, huh! Just look across the way at that ridge between us and the Fence. If you look long enough you will see patterns of shadows in the treetops that indicate, like a skeleton, there are multiple ribs rising to the highest elevation along the ridge, call it a backbone. Look long enough and you see that one of these ribs is but an extension of the backbone itself all the way to the bottom. Imagine you're trying to get on top of the backbone of someone lying down by climbing up one of its ribs. You may start off okay but eventually every possible rib takes a very steep rise as it turns to meet the backbone. That means lots of blasting to get through. Only a route that starts at the beginning of the backbone offers the longest run, hence, the flattest grade, meaning the least blasting. So, tell me Tom, which one of those ridge lines is the starting point of that hill's backbone? Which one is overall the least steep route all the way to the top?"

Looking more bemused than puzzled, Tom said admittedly, "Okay sir. So many secrets. So little interest. I will leave the mystery of siting the perfect mountain road to you and others. But sir, I AM a bit curious about one part of what you do out there. As I said, most of the time, without hesitation, you slapped down a flag for the 'dozer to follow. But some of the time you looked like you were just wandering around aimlessly, then you slowly placed the flag, still looking around making sure you were right. What is all that shuffling about?"

Daniel quickly responded, "It's the vegetation. The entire DMZ has returned to a wilderness state in full climax, the way it was before any humans stepped foot here. This place is mostly oaks, maples and birches, the natural fare. But what is a bit crazy, everything in this part of the DMZ is stunted because just under our feet is a massive expanse of decomposed and not so decomposed granite. Though each tree is a bit short, forcing us to keep our heads down, they have a grand interlocking canopy causing so much shade that nothing much grows underneath, so you can easily see how everything goes together."

Dan went on, "That's the easy stuff. Anyone can quickly grasp the lay of land to decide the highest point of the ridge along the route when it is so easy to see all around. But then you get to patches of hillside that are not easy. Tears in the universe. It could be due to wind thrown trees felled 10 years ago, opening the canopy, allowing direct sunlight to hit the ground, triggering a wide array of shrubs and leafy new growth blocking the way. A land slide from 50 years ago is now overgrown with weeds and scruff waiting for the soil's natural moisture content and compaction to return so that then, and only then, fully mature trees can grow to

                                                                                   Unremembered Victory

replace in-kind what was there before. These and other events expedite boundless arrays of dense vegetation that thrive in transitional, or as the textbooks call them, 'ruderal' areas. All around such places, site distance is no further than the tangle of foliage inches from your face. That's when you start finding your way more by touch than sight. The quest is to push through the bushes enough until you are satisfied you are on the true break point. That is the one, the only one place that is the highest spot along the ridge where, if you poured water on the ground, half would flow to the left and half to the right as you look up slope. Linked together, these points keep the dozer operator on the true crest of the ridgeline from one end to the other, offering the overall flattest grade requiring the least amount of blasting needed to get it to grade." (Grade in military parlance means a 2½ Ton Truck can pass (20 feet rise to 100 feet run) all the way up to the top and down without hesitation or mishap, rain or snow or ice.)

Tom responded, "Sir, that is a lot more than I need to know but interesting just the same."

Daniel then said, "The next three days we will be working the south side of the ridge between where we made grade and the Guard Post, a half mile away. According to my maps, this ridge is the highest ground in the DMZ, so a North Korean sniper could pick off our guys with ease from anywhere. Yes, that, and if you did not notice, the Military Demarcation Line (MDL) markers that divide North and South Kores are as little as 25 feet from a road along the crest. To not be so vulnerable, we are going to put the road a bit south, just below the ridgetop in defilade to hide the trucks from the North Koreans."

Tom said, "Okay. Good to know. That means we cannot be shot at from the North because this big ol' hill will be in the way."

Daniel then said to Tom, "Yes. That's what's in the Military Engineering Handbooks. By the way, talking about by the book, I got to tell you, you and your guys are amazing. Every day you put a five-man cordon around us. No one can get a shot on us without coming through you. You're on the deal all the time. And I swear every Imjin Scout I meet north of the River is the same. Who could imagine we could get this good this fast? It was not that long ago I dismissed the whole 2nd Infantry Division as a friendly fire contest."

The words 'friendly fire' set Tom impulsively wanting to remember his early days in theater. He opened by saying to Daniel, "You know, I remember my first day in Korea. I got here about the same time you did. Everyone was in a bit of a state, waiting to have their name called and be told the dice they had been thrown. Everyone had heard many stories from the local cadre addressing dangers awaiting any assigned to the Second Infantry Division. Of course, none of these desk jockeys knew anything first-hand and were only repeating what they had heard about 'Indian Country' referred to in ominous tones." Tom guessed that the roughest these guys had had it was of being served a warm Black Label beer at the NCO club.

Tom gave Dan a look and Dan gave Tom a look back that he was fine with wandering off the mandatory nonfraternization reservation. "You know, sir, I also remember at first being quite overwhelmed by sights and sounds of Korea but most vividly the smells. I grew up in rural America in the South. The smell reminded me of outside toilets I had used as a youngster when visiting my grandparents. They had never experienced running water or an inside bathroom, and certainly no telephone. Electricity was introduced to the community during the late 1940s. The house was loosely wired with single lines running into a few rooms and the light fixture dangled with a pull cord. Kerosene lamps were kept handy since they never knew when there would be an outage."

Tom went on to say, "Anyway, back to my early days here, my name was called eventually. I was being sent to the Second Infantry Division, along with 25 or so other guys. We were put aboard a full-size Army truck for the rumble up to 2ID headquarters. Boy, I remember what a ride that was, everyone so quiet, lost in thought, surveying the countryside, and wondering what might lie ahead. After all, each of us was headed into Indian Country, the 2ID insignia being a stoic Indianhead on a shield.

"When the trucks stopped, a Sergeant motioned us off the trucks telling us to bring our duffle bags. We were directed to the mess hall. Then he told us to assemble at the flagpole to learn our destinations. We lined up and collected our trays and glasses for the noon meal. It was an impressive menu. I soon learned that really good food was customary in most of the mess halls up north."

                                             Unremembered Victory

Tom continued, "Later around the flagpole I watched the local guys mill around. They didn't seem to be stressed and their bantering was mixed with laughter that made me feel more at ease. I thought that this will be a good assignment, right here. That feeling quickly evaporated when eventually my name was called, followed by being told I was assigned to the 1st/9th at Camp Custer, a location yet further north. It did not take long to be told it was a hard-core infantry regiment with their own special belt buckle that was formed into a dragon head. Then I heard stories about blown up Jeeps, fire fights, barracks satchel charged and ambushes; lots of ambushes."

Tom continued, "Hostile fire activity seemed to be picking up just in time for my arrival. Once at Camp Custer, I was assigned to B-Company, Captain Everett's command. I had just heard from a young PFC that Everett was a gung-ho and "Sorry I'm not in Vietnam" fire breathing bastard. My first encounter with Captain Everett he asked, "They keep sending me pieces of shit who I have to teach to be soldiers. Are you one of those pieces of shit, Specialist?" Having dealt with people like Everett all my life, I carefully measured his response, 'Suh, I am a class A dingleberry toting shit wad that specializes in shit, …I can stand on my head and spot shit from across a room and determine their last meal contents. Suh, shit so bad flies will land only with two of their little feet. Now that I am a determined an expert, where would you like for this shit wad to bunk, SUH.' Captain Everett smiled, eyes twinkling and responded, 'Carry on soldier. Shit as good as yours is directed to report to Lieutenant Chip, he'll be your commanding officer.'"

Tom went on, wanting Dan to know more about his life north of the River, "I caught a ride to Headquarters Company where I was told upon arrival that I was promoted to the CO's Jeep driver. I got to thinking 'damn that was quick'. Next thing I know I am moving across the River. Damn, just like that. Then the real scuttlebutt begins. I am informed that straws were drawn, and our fortune would be snuffing Joe, any North Korean spotted on our side of the MDL markers. I have got to tell you, Sir, I have been in 'Indian Country' on that mission ever since.

"THINK"
Aretha Franklin

Think (think) think (think) think (think)
Think (think) think (think) think (think)

You better think (think) think about what you're trying to do to me
Yeah, think (think, think), let your mind go, let yourself be free

Let's go back, let's go back, let's go way on way back when
I didn't even know you,

you couldn't have been too much more than ten. (just a child)
I ain't no psychiatrist, I ain't no doctor with degrees
It don't take too much high IQ's to see what you're doing to me

You better think (think) think about what you're trying to do to me
Yeah, think (think, think), let your mind go, let yourself be free

Oh freedom (freedom), freedom (freedom), freedom, yeah freedom
Freedom (freedom), freedom (freedom), freedom, ooh freedom

12

FOOD TO THE HUNGRY, WARMTH TO THE FREEZING
IS GENUINE RESPECT TO THE MARGINALIZED

The next day, after spending most of the day flagging the new road, Daniel was just stuck at Guard Post Bravo with a need to check up on his assigned surveyors at Guard Post Charlie about two miles away as the crow flies. The road trip from Charlie to Bravo was over an hour and Daniel had to wait for Simpson to return with the jeep from an errand that would take at least an hour more. Daniel had two choices. Hang out at the guard post, wait for the Simpson and by the time they were back out to the Barrier Road, it would be too late to take the long road to GP Charlie. There was a bit of urgency in meeting up with the surveyors since he was to give them new op orders for the coming week. It could wait but better they knew about it now. So, there was a second choice—cut cross country between the two guard posts.

Plan B started to wear on Dan. "Hell!" he thought, "What's this Imjin Scout business all about anyways. If I do not make this run, I may never know what it's like to be on patrol in the DMZ." Then he thought, "Hey! I can be my own point. What's does it matter if that's all there is if the point gets through. Besides, thought Dan, "I have my trusty 45 with which I cannot hit anything." Dan left word at the guard post to tell Simpson to pick him up at GP Charlie and set off across country.

Within minutes, Daniel found himself deep into the stunted oak forest prevalent along this part of the DMZ. To make the trek required traversing a series of low ridges and large swales with lots of sight distance to get off a round at an opponent, blocked by only sporadic tree trunks. The many oak trees presented a dense canopy of dead oak leaves still hanging onto every branch. In early March, there were still many expansive patches of old icy snow too big to walkaround that emanated loud popping sounds with each you-did-not know-which next step. The rest of the ground was covered in a carpet of fallen leaves, still crispy after months on the ground, giving every move quite a crunch crunch soundtrack. All that noise did not matter all that much since most of the time it was masked by wind rustling the dead brown leaves still clinging to thousands of branches on the trees that sounded like a low drum roll that masked out all other sound.

No question, as soon as Daniel was away from the GP, he could bump into an enemy patrol either on the move or stationery, as in an ambush. Since they were on our side of the Demarcation Line, their only interest was to hunt and kill GIs with handheld weapons and grenades. On the other hand, on our side of the Demarcation Line, we were allowed platoons of halftracks and tanks as backup. These were the DMZ rules stuck to by both sides, sans occasional unsanctioned use of machine guns on either side of the Line. They had AK47s. We fortunately were issued M14s, not M16s. Don't let that wooden stock fool you. Every man a sniper, and unlike the M16s in Vietnam, every gun never jammed.

Though not trained in these matters, not being an Imjin Scout, Daniel still had the good sense to stand motionless whenever the wind died down to hide his movement and listen for sounds made by the enemy. After proceeding patiently like that for a while, THERE! Dan was sure he heard something. The wind came up and the white noise of the crinkly leaves hid the sound of his feet and that of a possible enemy, again. Daniel moved on. The wind stopped. The ubiquitous vibration of the small brown oakleaves finally almost flatlined and Daniel was certain he had heard enough to feel he was being followed. Alone, with only his 45, what to do?

Daniel's mind raced around his head. What he learned in Basic; what he learned in OCS; none of that meant jack about what to do here. Daniel suddenly remembered the not widely known 'Bill Steinberg Which-Eye Negotiation'. He learned it from a close down-on-his-luck acquaintance, William Steinberg. Despite an excellent UCLA education and all the entitlements of a rich Westwood doctor's son, Bill found himself in a real-time George Orwell's Down and Out in Paris and London story. Working as a cab driver in Compton, Bill was having his ride taken from him by a large, very large person. Bill once explained to Daniel that having failed at every endeavor, he could not fail at being a cab driver, his next step for putting his life back together, or not. Instead of allowing the very big cab driver to usher his fare into the big guy's cab, Bill just lost it. He got out of his cab and stepped between the fare and the rear door of the big guy's cab and screamed,

"That is my fare and you will have to fight me to take it away from me."

At this point, Bill said, he was on a death wish as he screamed,

"But here are the rules. At the end of the fight I will be dead! No question you are way too good for me. However, you must ask yourself just one question. WHICH EYE are you going to lose before it's over?"

Much more to Bills' joy than surprise, the big cabby backed off bellowing that Bill was clearly CRAZY, out of his mind and while repeatedly reminding some corner of the cosmos that he did not fight crazy people, got in his cab and drove away.

Remembering this protocol, Daniel knew what to do. He waited for the wind to die down and took his 45 pistols out of its holster, inspected the clip in the handle and reinserted it, turned the safety off and readied the weapon to be cocked, chambering a round. Spring-loaded, the resulting sound is guaranteed the same every time. Daniel waited and waited until that rare moment when there was no wind at all, when it all died away, just when the enemy would be listening most attentively for his next step. Hold it. Hold it. Hold it until the absolute quietest moment… Hold it. Daniel rapidly chambered a round evoking a CLASTATERCHNAPPPkhaaah!!! sound that could be heard for miles. Whether the sound was lost on the trees or fell on the ears of his assailants, Daniel had what he needed most. He had given off the most important signal you can share with an opponent.

I AM NOT GOING TO BE EASY!

Daniel felt that he had regained enough control to decisively continue all the way to GP Charlie, which he did, in just over an hour as planned. Once he got clear of the sheer obsession of just staying alive, the beauty all around him once again brought to mind how untouched wilderness is like holy ground, where every tree and shrub is a burning bush on a sunny day after a rain when all the leaves shimmer.

There was a little hassle when approaching the ranks in positions around GP Charlie. Only Imjin Scouts were assigned radios. Combat Engineers could do just fine with face to face verbal exchanges like "Hey! I'm a friendly." In this instance, as Daniel so cautiously took each step so intently looking in every direction, he did not see three GIs on a break crouched down in the bushes not even 30 feet away until one of them derisively yelled out, "Hey! Get a load of John Wayne lost in the woods" There was no attempt to hide themselves, their olive-green uniforms doing the job and the naturally tangled flora of the DMZ doing the rest.

STUCK INSIDE OF MOBILE WITH THE MEMPHIS BLUES AGAIN
Bob Dylan

Oh, the ragman draws circles
Up and down the block
I'd ask him what the matter was
But I know that he don't talk
And the ladies treat me kindly
And they furnish me with tape
But deep inside my heart
I know I can't escape
Oh, Mama
Can this really be the end?
To be stuck inside of Mobile
With the Memphis blues again

Unremembered Victory

13

WILDERNESS REVELATIONS ARE NOT SIGNS FROM HEAVEN. YOU ARE ALREADY THERE. SIGNS ARE EVERYWHERE YET TO BE SEEN

The next day, Daniel and Brune collected Tom and his four other squad members, 3 GIs and 2 KATUSA. As before, Tom's rifle team formed a perfect cordon around Daniel and Brune as they worked the hill. As he and Brune moved to place the next flag, they moved like ballet around them. On lunch break, with the officer-noncom thing out the way, Daniel hunkered down next to Tom to shoot the shit.

"You know", Daniel started off, "While at Ft Belvoir OCS, I found among all the OCS Candidates the ones from military families the most tragic. There were two things they knew for sure. This was their war AND they had to go to Vietnam to test their mettle and make rank. They also knew EVEN by '67 that upon stepping out of the plane onto the tarmac, they would be dirty for the rest of their lives, complicit with an obscenity, tar they would never get entirely off."

Daniel continued, "The most afraid I can ever remember being were the five months of OCS. It was only the winter of 67' and already the reports were coming in from Vietnam of friendly fire killing of officers by their own men for being, as they saw it, giving hard orders [had to be obeyed]. This made perfect sense to me, having encountered PROGRAM 100,000 troops in boot camp. The dumb ones were disconcerting, but the ones scraped out of the bottom of the mental health or criminal justice system were real scary. Drawn to violence, three of them one Sunday afternoon systematically cornered and threatened to cut the throat of at least a dozen GIs, me included, just for the fun of it. I laughed my way loose since the whole thing seemed too funny not to laugh or I made it that way. No one turned in a complaint, dismissing the situation as joking around the regular troops had to put up with.

"That these guys were in the ranks in Vietnam was not lost on me. Every morning I would wake up with this 'taste' in my mouth like I had been sucking on a battery all night. Breakfast, for what little food I got to eat, barely phased it. Took until about 10:30 AM or so for it to fade away. Cold steely fear, that's what that taste was. Fear I would get my commission, go to Vietnam, give hard orders and be fragged by my own men, OR, shave points to stay alive. Either way, I would not get home alive."

Tom said, "So what about right now. Here we are north of the Fence right in the middle of the Action Jackson where I hear we lost 2 yesterday not a thousand yards from here. What about that?"

Daniel said, "I will tell you Tom. When I first got to Korea, like you, I was scared to even be in Seoul since there are infiltrators everywhere forcing a shoot-to-kill curfew. Just being outside after 10:00 PM was deadly. You know, caught in crossfire anywhere anytime.

"But I thought to myself, at least I am in Seoul and not up north. Then I was assigned up north and I thought, now I am up north but I'm not north of the Imjin River in the DMZ.

"Then I ran my first recon in the DMZ and thought I may be in the DMZ, but at least I am not north of the Fence.

"And then I was ordered to do recon north of the Fence for the first time, and as I went through the gate, thought, 'Hey, this is slick.'"

Tom said, "I totally agree with you. There were no longer any unknowns. By being in the most dangerous possible situation, a bit of control returns. That's what I've learned out here. What we all yearn for most is CON-TROL, having a lot of say over what happens next. So, going through the gate liberates me from dread of even greater unknown danger, causing fear to melt away to 'feeling ready'—sometimes more ready than other times."

Daniel added, "Speak of control, I guess it helps to know how much we trust the Korean troops assigned to us. Nice kids, so totally loyal, we have to work hard to be as good as them."

Tom blurted out, "Trusted. It's so much bigger than that. Talk about the right fight… Here I will show you. Raising his voice, a bit, Tom cheerfully called out, Hey Cho! Chu Sung, how about get your butt over here" One of the KATUSA soldiers quickly jogged forward. "Hey, Cho. Tell the Lieu-tenant what you think of America?"

"Oh! Whotenant Shawkawitz", Cho gleefully chimed in. "America Number 1. Without America, we part of China. You die. We die. Truth never die. It just get covered up - so many lies, cannot see it. It there just the same. It never stop. Like how everyone so much the same. You guys get along so well is so crazy, like one people out of many different people. Easy for us. Only one kind of Korean. Korean. Every Korean no matter where they are from. There are no Italian Koreans, French Koreans. We all just Koreans. One blood, that's easy. You Americans. So much harder, so many kinds of people. The more Koreans understand how Americans get along with each other, learn to believe in each other like you guys do, stronger we become. Maybe we become like America, big house, nice cloths, maybe car, not just dirt roads."

Daniel laughed, "Hey Cho, you talk so well, you're so polite and so modest considering your talents. Come to think it, most all of you KATUSAs fit your mold. How did you wind up here?"

Cho said, "That easy. Family business class. Have connections. Know who to pay, so here I am."

Daniel inquired. "What do you mean pay?"

Cho said, "All Korean men must serve. KATUSA in the US sector of DMZ we get to learn best American English."

Daniel reminded Cho, "But of the entire 135-Mile-long zone, these 18 miles are the traditional invasion route to Seoul. Our sector is by far the most dangerous, you could be killed any second, for what?"

Cho said, "Small price to pay to learn good English. I know sound crazy, how everything so primitive and poor now, but Koreans believe better days soon and we think America best rabbit to chase to better life."

Dan loved being witness to the enthusiasm of his Army's integrated troops program, Korean Augmentation Troops USA [KATUSA]. Truly understanding our deal by being among us, to them, was worth dying for. And we, thanks to Cold War School, did not disappoint. Defection and AWAL rate nationwide were ZERO. Dan could not stop thinking about the ridiculous contrast between his military experience in the 2ID and the news from Vietnam.

There was one tiny incident that really put Dan just over the top. He had started dropping by from time to time to RC (Recreation Area) 3. Kind of nuts, the librarian was a matronly woman, Department of the Army Civilian. How she so miraculously was there every time Dan dropped by was a mystery that Dan chose not to ponder. First, he checked out books and records. Then he ordered stuff. After a time or two, when he ordered a copy of Prokofiev's 'The Love for Three Oranges', the librarian mentioned it would be there for pick-up the day after next. Daniel said that would be great because he was scheduled to be back up on the Line and could drop by. Daniel did just that on his way south two days later and there it was. Still in pristine shrink wrap, its classy cover staring back at him.

That night, Daniel broke the seal and placed the untouched record on his Gerard Turntable and played it on his Pioneer stereo while thinking, "How the hell did the Army do it?" All there was back then were punch cards. How could they put an order into Japan, attain the record, have it shipped to Korea, and then somehow get it all the way up to inside the DMZ in two days. He just could not stop thinking how this simple but miraculous act so completely exemplified the attitude of everyone on the Line and supporting the Line. People could just not do enough for each other. Near to a man or woman, to different degrees, everyone figured out what they could do to improve the mission and just did it, anything that increased the comfort and security of the next person.

Casualties flat lined by end of Summer, and but for a spike or two, the last of which was March '69, after the Pueblo crew was returned the prior December. After that, all went silent on the Line and there has not been a lethal shot fired since. More importantly, North Korea abandoned its long-time effort to subvert South Korea into becoming a part of North Korea, enabling South Korea to rocket from sticks and mud into a 1st World power, once it got clear of its primary need being just internal security.

THE MIGHTY QUINN (QUINN THE ESKIMO)
Manfred Mann

Come all without, come all within
You'll not see nothing like the mighty Quinn
Come all without, come all within
You'll not see nothing like the mighty Quinn

Everybody's building ships and boats
Some are building monuments, others are jotting down notes
Everybody's in despair, every girl and boy
But when Quinn the Eskimo gets here everybody's gonna jump for joy

Come all without, come all within
You'll not see nothing like the mighty Quinn

14

KIND ACTS TREAT ALL INVOLVED AS OF THE SAME KIND

The next day of flagging the road, while Daniel and Tom were talking on lunch break, Daniel suddenly blurted, "Hey! I'm issued only a 45! I can't hit a damn thing with it, it kicks up on me and I wind up not even able to hit you and you're only 6 feet away. You have an M14. With an M14, even I can hit a bullseye at 1000 feet. As a Combat Engineer, I am expected to return fire. That I will most likely not hit anything is okay with me. You know how quick I am at the ready with pistol out and safety off. Simply the which-eye negotiation I mentioned earlier. They know I am going to get a round off. They have no idea what a bad shot I am. You know, I am only out here because my Southern upbringing demands it. As for me, backing the bad guy down short of lethal force I think is plenty compliance enough."

There was a long serene pause all around, followed by Tom getting off a new thought, glad that LT. Schikevitz was up for receiving it. "As I see it, there is a reason for this. As a history nut, right here, right now is so far ahead of anything that ever came before. Before America, the world was 7,000 years of wall-to-wall different flavors of mafia setups, total power from the top to the bottom with a don at the top and everyone else somewhere in the heap with prospects of being allowed to move up or down a click or two, but not much else. This is so different. Each of us deciding for ourselves what we will do next, not someone else. Seven generations later, HOLY SHIT! It still works! Of course, here we have no free will at all, a small price to pay for what's up ahead.

Dan had worked the South side of the ridge until he was satisfied that where he had placed each flag would result in the least amount of side-hill cut and fill that would be required to keep the trucks in defilade. Since things were wrapping up, Dan decided to dig into Tom's psyche a bit more before they disengaged. "Okay Tom", "said Daniel, "Let's talk about you. I've watched. There is no shirk in you. You just do it and you do it 100%" Daniel asked Tom, "So what makes you so quick to do it?"

"Sir, I have heard you say how you are going back to California to start from zero and see how far you can get. Well for me, I have the same feeling, but I come from so little, I feel like I have covered a lot of ground already. But it has not been rosy. My mom had a knack for marrying men who did okay at first and then fell apart. As it goes, at fifteen I started being the bread winner around the house, working lots of hours at a nearby supermarket all during high school. Can't complain. Gave me a fire in my belly that put me in Community College and my third stripe in this Army. But it has come at a price of being an outlier, not able to run with the popular kids, but popular enough to know that I could if I had the time. Hell. The high school had fraternities and sororities, so you were either in or out. Your family has the money to cover dues and labels in your clothes and you were in. I felt fine with that crowd just the same."

TO SIR WITH LOVE
Lulu, Samantha Mumba

The time has come for closing books and long last looks must end
And as I leave I know that I am leaving my best friend
A friend who taught me right from wrong and weak from strong
That's a lot to learn, but what can I give you in return?
If you wanted the moon, I would try to make a start
But I would rather you let me give my heart 'To Sir, With Love'

15
WHAT ARE THE TWO SPEEDS OF ART?
TRUTH AND WAITING

Colonel Miller held three parties for the 2nd Combat Engineer Officers during Daniel's tour. All three were the same. For the sake of the morale, attendance was mandatory. To assure this, individual orders were cut for every officer in the Battalion, except the officer of the day. He, and only he, was exempt. There were always some girls brought in from the village near the entrance of Battalion Headquarters. They were all $2 short time, so it was not uncommon for the interested to engage the same or different girl more than once in the same night. BUT the centerpiece of the Colonel's party was the bar. For those not interested in displaying their private life in front of everyone, most of the officers were wallowing in a different kind of testosterone driven sentiment—competition. Here's how it worked. At every Colonel's party, the tab was split among the attendees with the Colonel paying for three shares, Line officers 2 shares and the rest, one share each. When the bar opened at exactly 7 PM, there was only one universal thought at work. I am getting drunk on their dime; they're not getting drunk on mine. That required absolutely no distractions from binge drinking, like going back to your billet for a 'short time'. Sunday morning after the Colonel's first party, Dan woke up in his bed still wearing his dress wool fatigues intact. He remembered the bar, a lot of loud banter, a lull while the Colonel made a short speech and then more loud banter. Daniel could not remember leaving the party. He could not remember how he got back to his billet just 200 feet away from the Officer's Club. He could not remember how he got to bed still fully clothed. AND he had no idea why there were huge holes in his fatigues around the knees. The worse part was no one would tell him what happened—not his bunkmate, the other officers, the waiters and bar tenders at the Officer's Club and not even the house boys, who knew everything about everything. All that remained a mystery until the next Colonel's party some three months later. Dan was so much wiser now. He knew better how to pace his drinking to stay on the right side of black outs. And then it was 7:00 PM, the bar opened.

                                                      Unremembered Victory

The next morning, Daniel found himself back in bed with all his clothes on and gaping holes in the knees of his pants. Again, no one would tell him what happened, this time their stares tinged with just a smidge of impatient mirth.

Dan rode out the rest of his DMZ tour without ever getting closer to the truth other than the obvious deduction that since every billet had a four-foot bed of crushed gravel around it for drainage purposes, crawling aimlessly around there is not good for your pants.

When the Colonel threw the 3rd Party, Dan did not go. He paid the designated officer of the day $20 to go in his stead, had his orders altered and was off the hook. Dan was also a bit flusher for all the fuss since the bar tab for a Lieutenant ran over $35 for a drunk that Dan had learned the easy way, he did not want any more.

THERE IS A MOUNTAIN
Donovan

First there is a mountain, then there is no mountain, then there is
First there is a mountain, then there is no mountain, then there is
The caterpillar sheds his skin to find a butterfly within
Caterpillar sheds his skin to find a butterfly within
First there is a mountain, then there is no mountain, then there is
First there is a mountain, then there is no mountain

16

LETTING HATE DEFINE YOU LONG ENOUGH
RUNS THE RISK OF BECOMING NOTHING BUT EMBODIED HATE
AND YOU'RE NOT THERE AT ALL

As Daniel approached, the survey crew was setting up and recording road alignments to the guard post in the background far away. Firefights were heard in a distance. Some sounded like just a nervous GI unloading a clip in the bushes. Occasionally there was the more muffled sound of a grenade fired by a launcher. When Daniel arrives at the site, he saw with great relief that all was right. All were smiling and motioning to their flak jackets, helmets on their heads, and most amazing by their side, their M14 with clip in, safety on. Everyone was beaming, huge smiles, ear to ear, everyone.

Daniel exhaled, "What a relief! It was only a matter of time the North Koreans selected you for their next bozos-don't-shoot-back hit. Seven at the ready, I would say you are no longer a target of choice, one they will pass up for easier pickin's. No lifetime grieving for me."

Sam beamed, "I must admit that trying to do it all seems to feel a whole lot better than bullshitting everybody. We have talked it over and we have all agree. Even if we are hit and killed, you can count on us to do our best to being found with a warm gun."

Suddenly, quite a distance away there was heard a sound something different, loud and sustained. Daniel exclaimed, "Did you hear THAT?"

Above the white noise of sporadic firefights was the distinct ACK ACK sound of a heavier weapon, something heavier than they had both ever heard before.

SAM screamed, "MOUNTED FIFTIES! FUUUUUCKK!"

Now they were breaking down the survey gear and nearly throwing it in the ¾ ton truck and all seven surveyors and Daniel piled into the truck and started racing to the fire.

Daniel yelled, "MOUNTED FIFTIES! MOUNTED FIFTIES!"

Sam screamed, "FUUUCKK!" In unison they wailed together, "MOUNTED FIFTIES!"

The truck violently slid through a tight turn in the road. Why slow down. The truck was now on only two wheels, on its way to rolling over. On the way to the tipping point, perhaps a Korean trait not shared with the GIs, the three KATUSAS instinctively threw their bodies to the other side of the truck and the whole thing teetered for more seconds than you want to count. The whole time in the turn, without missing a beat, everyone still screaming…

"MOUNTED FIFTIES! FUUUUUUCKKKK! MOUNTED FIFTIES!"

The truck came skidding into the guard post area just in time to hear the last shots fired. Dan could barely see what was going on, the air was so choked with dust. Pebbles were raining down out of the sky.

SAM screamed, "Damn. Missed the whole thing!"

Daniel said, "And it was a big one. Hey, I know this guy strutting toward us. He is the platoon leader here."

The 1st LT. in-charge was coming toward them with huge strides and a boundless smile on his face that seemed to consume his very being. He was waving and greeting while repeatedly glancing up over his right soldier at where the North Korean Guard post used to be across the ravine. Then without breaking stride he looked at us and bellowed. "Holy shit. They were STRAFFING US. In the DAYTIME!"

Daniel yelled, "Where in hell is the guard post? I have been looking up at their dug in bunkers and fortifications for months, staring down on us and now they're GONE!"

Scanning at the northern horizon, your eyes slowly came to rest on some scattered upright fragments of what used to be a North Korea fortification.

The Platoon Leader said, "Yeah. The quad 50s did it. After so many minutes of enemy fire, I said, 'fuck it' and ordered up the armor. And they sent them! And they got here right away. See. Two of them, a total 8 mounted 50 caliber machine guns in all. They just worked that ridge and then whatever was causing all this grief was just no more!"

Daniel yelled out at the sky, "DAMN! And we missed the whole thing. Look at them up there. You can see light reflecting off shiny surfaces as they mill about the wreckage of what a minute ago was their guard post. AND WE MISSED IT!"

The Infantry Lieutenant said, "Hey. Cheer Up. You have a new medal to wear in your head for the rest of your life - 'I ran to the fire.'"

DANCE TO THE MUSIC
Sly and the Family Stone

Dance to the Music, dance to the music
All we need is a drummer
For people who only need a beat
I'm gonna add a little guitar
And make it easy to move your feet
I'm gonna add some bottom
So that the dancers just won't hide
You might like to hear my organ
I said ride Sally ride

17

SINCE THE DMZ DEFENDERS HAD BEEN RANOMLY SELECTED, SWAP IN ANY RANDOMLY SELECTED 4,000 SOLDIERS IN VIETNAM AND THE RESULT WOULD HAVE BEEN JUST THE SAME

Not long after that, Daniel was out flagging the road again with Tom and his five-man cordon around him. Again, Tom and Daniel fell to speculating over lunch, with Dan opening with, "Just being here makes you realize what an obscenity Vietnam is in comparison, perhaps worse than we know. Think about it. Here we are, four months out of Tet and it looks like the Paris Peace Talks are changing the story from victory to just keeping the fighting going on and on. Like we have not lost until we are made to quit. The perfect cash-cow. Years of insanely huge defense profits followed by expected defeat."

Tom said, "So why not just drop the bombs in the ocean. The profits to the defense contractors would be the same."

Dan smirked, "Oh Tom, you just don't get it. The bombs must be dropped on people for the streaming gratuitous killing of innocence to crush the core values of all who serve there."

Tom said, "So big deal, a bunch of guys get their heads screwed up. IF I get out of here, what I think about America will be just outrageously terrific in my mind forever."

Daniel blurted out, "Hey! Do the numbers. There are just 10M American guys in our age group. If Vietnam goes on for three or more years at around 500,000 a click, then three million plus of us will have served there, nearly 1 in 3 of all of us will become distressed goods, not what we were when we come back, less able than our parents to fend off the excesses of power—90% tax rate on the rich INDEED! All that money going everywhere instead of just to the top.

Now, what do we have? You have seen it yourself. Returnees coming back dark from all the lies, friendly fire fatalities and complete collapse of trust. The next thing we know, our entire generation is just a bunch of

B-Listers, second-raters, with far less of the self-belief in the country and themselves that enabled our parents to deliver the affluent 50's and early 60's, when everyone got a piece of a market that kept exploding from everyone getting a piece of it."

As the day descended into dusk, increasing sounds of sporadic weapon fire began to fill the air. Tom told Daniel, "Me and my guys have to go. Our day is just starting. On patrol, all night. As for all this shooting, regular stuff about this time of day. I suggest, Sir, not going home until it subsides. Meanwhile, you can park yourself and your Jeep driver in that warmup hooch over yonder."

Daniel and Simpson, his assigned Jeep driver of the day, entered a small comfortable half buried lean-to structure with a stove and some boxes to sit on. Within minutes, a seven-man rifle squad of 2 KATUSAs and 5 GIs suddenly poured into the hooch. They looked bone tired and cold and quickly dispersed themselves around the room. They turned up the stove and two of them put some C Rations on the cover to heat them up. The others simply went limp, happy to be in a warm amiable situation rather than out on patrol on such a cold windy night. Daniel and Simpson were all but ignored. Meanwhile, the intensity and nearness of the shooting became ever greater until a thudding sound of bullets hitting the outside earth walls of the dugout could be discerned. Though the 2 KATUSAs showed some polish, the five GIs were just guys, as ordinary as you could imagine. One African, one Mexican and three European Americans all equally forgettable in demeanor. The next thing through the door might well have been North Korean commandos with AK 47s, busting into the room and killing everyone. Daniel and Simpson put a round in the chamber of their weapons and turned the safety off. They did not notice the others doing the same. Suddenly, an Infantry officer's face slammed through the door screaming, "What the Fuck are you doing in here. We are under ASSAULT. Move out! Move out! MOVE OUT! NOWWWWWW!"

Just as fast, he disappeared into the night. The seven, for just an instant, made eye contact all around, merging into a now standard communal look of 'We've got to do this but-nobody-gets-hurt-tonight'. Gear was instantly gathered, C-rations off the stove and they hit the entrance, one against the other, until all, in a whoosh, were out the door. Within seconds, the shooting got louder, with a tight staccato of rifle shots and clips being emptied. The shooting started getting further away as the enemy was repulsed. As the shooting got very far away, Daniel said to Simpson, "Time to go home."

PURPLE HAZE
The Jimi Hendrix Experience

Purple haze, all in my brain
Lately things they don't seem the same
Actin' funny, but I don't know why
Excuse me while I kiss the sky

18

**FOUR CORNERS IS A TRICKY SET OF 900-FOOT HIGH
MEADOW CAPPED PROMONTORIES PLUNGING DEEP DOWN
INTO MUIR WOODS
GORGEOUS TO LOOK AT. CAN'T KEEP GOING BACK
TO RAVINES SO LARGE THEY KNOW YOUR NAME
BUT YOU CANNOT KNOW THEIRS**

After Tom left Daniel at the warmup hooch, his rifle team joined up with another to form a 10-man squad to go out on ambush detail. Based on enemy sightings in the daytime and other clues of enemy activity, Tom had been told to take the squad out to the side of a small ridge overlooking a streamway often used as passage by the North Korean infiltrators. Everyone had already been on duty for eight hours and were expected to do 16 more before returning to their barracks. Ambush duty would continue until daylight.

About the enemy, Tom remembered the first time he heard a newly arrived GI in the ranks refer to the North Korean soldiers as Gooks. There was an instant mental recoil among all who heard it. Many quickly informed the newcomer that the preferred word was 'Joe', as in when Joe Jumps (invades). Like us, all during the conflict, North Korea honored the 1st Korean War Armistice Agreement, maintaining the same number of troops on their side that were on ours. One huge difference was that if one of them were wounded, GI's held back approaching the body until after the inevitable 'KROoom' of the grenade going off, committing suicide rather than suffer the dishonor of being captured.

When Tom wasn't on the Line, he would hang out in B Company area where it was impossible to stop listening nightly for the sounds of exploding claymores, the hiss of flares and weapons fire and the occasional exploding grenade. He knew these sounds came from nervous GIs blowing the shinola out of shadows that on occasion would be enemy combatants. Then there was the roar of the halftracks scurrying about, reposting troops to the hot areas. Tom put on a good show of quiet control in front of LT. Schikevitz, with his casual concern about the possibility of instant death from a sniper's bullet or possible enemy engagement north of the Fence. That was easy. They were only out there together in

                                   Unremembered Victory

the daytime, light duty compared to the nighttime, playtime for Joe's elite commandos.

And then there was the most dreaded sound of all that no one on the Line could stop listening for whenever there was a lot of activity— Libby Bridge and Freedom Bridge being blown up to impede the advancing horde.

Whenever there were sounds of a lot of firefights real or imagined, Tom would taste fear and see it in the eyes of his fellow GIs. Each would ask the other for their opinion about what the enemy was up to. When it was Tom's turn, he just pushed out the first hot air that entered his head like, "Just probing. Joe's looking for a weak link."

When enemy activity would crescendo, growing sounds of combat all up and down the Line caused the first thought in Tom's head was, "Has the clock started? Do we still have 15 minutes between when the invasion starts, Joe jumps, and the bridges are blown?" Of course, that will leave 4,000 GIs north of the Imjin River with no way south, to face the advancing horde alone. Worse, their orders were not to give up one foot of ground, the better to make the enemy mass on top of them to create a tight nuclear target. Arguably, such morbid orders contributed a lot to the lollygag before The Pueblo. Why care about anything when everyone else sure as hell didn't care about them, officially designated totally expendable. Of course, all that changed when General Izenour came roaring on the scene, making everyone too busy figuring out how to avoid their next reprimand to have any time to feel sorry for themselves.

Camp life routine changed after the Pueblo. Before, guys would be playing cards in the dayroom or writing letters home. What was being served in the mess hall was a big topic of the day with the unit being well fed calling for daily exercise to keep their weight down. Things were different now, the mood was a mixture of fear, anticipation, and excitement.

With a couple of months since General Izenour relieved the Bird Colonel on the spot, Tom had grown proud of his unit, proud how they had gone from I-could-give-shit-about-anything to each man's first concern being 'What's the mission? What's the procedure?' Down to a gnat's eyebrow. He liked the combination of got to do it but staying alive mattered more.

This combination led to procedures so tight that it came true even when being engaged in the most intense lethal combat. Complete commitment to the wellbeing of the next guy, their needs, safety and trust he found universal 'North of the River'.

When Tom did have a little free time, he returned to his hooch for a quick nap, and with the nap came dreams and memories. He dreamt about home and the woods out back with fondness, listening to the sounds and smelling the smells. Growing up, Tom became an avid hunter, mostly small game that made pretty good table fare. Many would jest when they heard his stories about squirrel hunting. But the squirrels he hunted weren't like the critters you see in a park, noisy and usually squabbling. Wild squirrels were wily and smart. Hunting them with success was a challenge.

This night, Tom had a recurring dream that he is hunting with his cousin. Quietly they approach a huge hickory tree, a giant that reach to the sky. There are several of the tiny beasts cracking and eating nuts, oblivious to their approach. Tom motions his cousin to stay put while he slips round the tree to the far side. Boom! The first shot sounds out and a squirrel falls mortally wounded. Another shot and another squirrel. The rest of the critters frantically scrambled as the boys began to reload to shoot again. Diligence

From the very top of the tree there is one lone squirrel looking down at them, seeming to say, 'Your shotgun can't reach this high'. Tom fires any-way. A few pellets get the squirrel's attention and in retaliation, squirrel leaps from the top of tree, dive bombing straight at Tom's head. Frozen at the thought of the squirrel hitting him smack in the face, Tom swings his shotgun like a bat, knocking the squirrel senseless. Casually Tom picks up the 'dead' squirrel and places it in his hunting vest pouch. His cousin says, "Nice hit Tom" and they continue to gather up the harvest. The hunt continues but after a short time Tom feels frenzied activity in his hunting vest. "Mercy", Tom exclaims as he franticly takes off his vest, yelling to his cousin, "Help me Ralph. This thing is eating me alive!" But Ralph is too busy rolling on the ground laughing uncontrollably to help. Just as Tom extricates the now fighting mad squirrel from his vest and pounds it against a tree, breaking bones and making the meat uneatable, he is SUDDENLY awake due to Gilliland, the Canadian, yelling,

                                                          Unremembered Victory

"Wakeup Tom, LT. Flynty needs your ass to tell him what to do."

Tom rubbed the sleep from his eyes and smiled at the Gilliland's familiar face and said,

"Gilliland, you Canadian piece of shit. If you had not stayed in Los Angeles so long you would not have to be here. Man! You had it made. You should have slipped back North of the border."

Gilliland, the Company Clerk, was an affable guy that never seemed to get down in the dumps, despite being north of the river, but at least not on patrol. Some cute girl had sent him the latest Beatles Album Sergeant Pepper 'something', and he played it on his portable record player over and over and ... Tom chuckled as he recalled the album came with a homemade Christmas card featuring Snoopy dancing, proclaiming "Merry Fucking Christmas." Tom asked Gilliland if he wanted to go out tonight and see the Z up close and personal? Gilliland smirked and replied,

"I'll leave that shit to you heroes…., remember I'm Canadian and we don't believe in any of this shit you Americans have come up with. But I do have to admit that this fight, the way we are fighting, does make sense. All in all, I will stay right here and you 'Keep Up the Fire.'"—[The tag line of his infantry regiment]s.

Tom grabbed his gear and left the hooch with the sounds of Ringo Starr singing some dumb ass song about being 64 and someone still loving him. At 23:30 Tom entered the Orderly Room to find LT. Flynt nervously pacing about checking and re-checking his radio. "Sir, Tom implored, "Are we ready to mount up?" A moment of pause and the young LT. responded that he needed a headcount, "Don't want to come back with fewer than when we started."

Tom responded with an affirmative. LT. Flynt was new and an obviously nervous. He was the last in his class at OCS, but none of the men knew that, however they could guess. His new name was LT. Clueless, but never to his face. His gold bars gleamed on his starched fatigues, having not had the where with all to replace the reflective brass bar with an embroidered black thread one. Better his bar stood out since his rank needed to be known. Otherwise he might have been confused for an E-2.

"Mount up men," he barked in his best command voice, "We've got a job to do." From the rear you could hear a mumble from one of the Short Timers who 'used to be' a Short Timer since everyone was officially extended beyond the normal 396 days since The Pueblo Seizure. There were two Jeeps and the ¾ ton in the convoy, no lights and dark as a cave. Somehow Tom was in the vehicle that was to lead the way. It was very cold, windy, and dark. It was a moonless overcast night and the road leading to the barrier Fence was so dark that at 5 mph it seemed like one was speeding. Suddenly the old ¾ ton sputtered, coughed, and died. Tom tried to coax it back to life, but she was a goner, all the new trucks were in Vietnam. "Shit, this sucks?" Tom thought.

All dismounted to survey the situation and offer remedies, but no good resolution was achieved for the ¾ ton. LT. Flynt was very persistent that all mount the two Jeeps and continue to the assignment. Tom wound up being left behind to guard a ¾ Ton, dead in it tracks, in the dark with no back up. "What the hell, "he thought. "I'm in the middle of a dark road, meters from the Debarkation Line, enemy combatants making their way south, 5 magazines of ammo and alone, very alone." After the noise of the vehicles went silent Tom realized what being truly alone felt like. A twig would snap or a thump from a tree branch hitting the ground would cause his mind to create hostilities with a ton of Joes coming at him. He tried to block these thoughts out of his mind, but it was impossible. He had never felt so alone and vulnerable. Tom locked and loaded his M14 and clicked the safety off thinking, "If they come, I'll have to fight like hell!"

Next, he heard an M-60 sporadically firing, intertwined with the sounds of M-14s. When a Claymore exploded, he hit the dirt. He thought "Damn they are on top of me." When the flares from the 4.2 mortar exploded over his head it created a daylight view. He realized he was in the open with no cover. "My God," Tom muttered, "I've got to get in a more defensive position." He saw a sandbag bunker and when the flare had extinguished. He felt his way to it. Entering it made him feel more secure, but his mind was still racing, creating scenarios of Rocket Propelled Grenades coming right at him, or a frontal attack with AK 47 rifles blazing.

The real firing continued and then down the Line a new burst of shooting from a different position. He thought, "Have my guys been caught in an ambush, did they hit a mine.

The enemy didn't come, his M-14 was placed back on safety and his heart rate slowed to nearly normal as daylight came. Things slowed down. In the east, he could see the light of the sun rising. Slowly the sun crept up the horizon until shadows disappeared, and the trees that were once combatants became trees again. A bird sang its morning song and Tom thought "Welcome to the land of the morning Calm." He heard a vehicle approaching and it was some friendlies coming back from their post. He waved them down and in very little time was whisked away from the land of lethal fire back to his hooch to hunker down and get ready to go out again in just a 24 hours.

WITH A LITTLE HELP FROM MY FRIENDS
John Lennon, Paul McCartney

What would you think if I sang out of tune,
Would you stand up and walk out on me?
Lend me your ears and I'll sing you a song
And I'll try not to sing out of key,
Oh, I get by with a little help from my friends, Mm,
I get high with a little help from my friends,
Mm, I'm going to try with a little help from my friends.

19

ADVANCE ALL OR SOME AT THE EXPENCE OF NONE

Daylight the next day found Daniel at the road construction site. Sounds of drilling could be heard over the din of big trucks carrying armed GIs. Shortly, the word was out. They were going to blast. Men ran and walked fast, deep into the woods, while some gathered with Daniel under a truck.

The blast Sergeant yelled his loudest,

"Fire in the Hole. Fire in the Hole. Fire in the Hole!"

A HUGE explosion went off for a good 10 seconds, causing a billowy brown plume of pulverized airborne dirt punctuated by streaking shards of jagged stone, each on its own wild trajectory. The sound of the blast blotted out all other existence. Men under the truck shielded their eyes to have a limited view of the spectacle. Lots of dirt and pebbles rained down.

As the dust cleared, Daniel was flanked by two 5 stripers, Master Sergeants Kent and Rodriquez. They both had too little time left in the Army until retirement to muster out, so were considered lifers, there for the pension. However, retiring with as much rank as possible, short of going to Officer Candidate School, made them up to task, whatever it was. No question they were serious about the Army, willing to face the enemy and quick to order their men out with them in front. Once the force and fury of the blast had subsided, Sergeant Rodriguez spotted something far more furious and foreboding than the side of a mountain being blown up - a Huey Helicopter inbound, already close enough to see that it had two white stars inside a red rectangle on its side. It could mean only one thing. General Izenour was coming in.

Rather than get ready for the visit, the two sergeants fell to arguing over who had more rank? Who was not going to have to face the general? This angst abruptly ended when it dawned on Rodriguez that neither of them needed to face the General, realizing that since LT. Schikevitz was clearly the ranking officer, he could do it alone. Where upon, yelling over their shoulders at Daniel that he was on his own, they both ran, literally ran, into the woods and were soon out of sight. Daniel's first thought was,

                                    Unremembered Victory

"Amazing. I had no idea those guys could run that fast." His next thought was, "Holy Shit! He is already out of his helicopter and heading up the hill." Daniel faced the general with the best full brace salute he had. The distance between them rapidly shrank to less than three feet. Long before that, Izenour was already screaming at the top of his lungs,

"How long before this fucking road will be finished?"

Daniel yelled back,
"I cannot speak for the whole battalion, SIR!"

General Izenour instantly shot back,
"Cut the crap you little shit, how long!"

Daniel bellowed short of spitting out a lung,
"FIVE WEEKS, SIR!"

Before the 'SIR' had passed Dan's lips, General Izenour had already turned and walked most of the way back to the Huey. As the Huey lifted off, Daniel, who had been saluting for a minute or so, forlornly dropped his salute that was not going to be returned.

After the General left, the Sergeants came back out of the forest and huddled with Daniel and asked if it were possible to be finished that soon.

Daniel said, "We have two more days of blasting to bring it to grade. You guys have done great. I was not sure we had the juice to obliterate that much granite, period. So, the iffy part is over but there are a lot of small jobs ahead, side hill cuts needed to keep the road hidden from the North. It can be done that fast. It will be a push, but push is what you guys do, and now you know the General is watching."

Once back at 2nd Combat Engineer HQ, Daniel reported to Captain McDowell what happened. McDowell made no comment other than insisting that Daniel tell it directly to the Colonel. Next thing Daniel knew he was standing in front of Colonel Miller in the middle of the Colonel's billet. Everyone was smiling while Daniel told them every detail of the encounter, except not having his salute returned. Now they were all smiling real smiles but otherwise standing there like Daniel was not quite done. With no comment coming, Daniel blurted, "So how did I do?"

McDowell remained silent but Colonel Miller, fighting to repress a smile, asked, "Five weeks huh?"

Daniel nodded agreement and Colonel Miller's body language indicated the meeting was over. He dismissed Daniel with a quiet, "You did fine." The Colonel was not in on it, having arrived after the 6 Day War, but Captain McDowell flashed Daniel 'the motion.'

Two weeks went by and Daniel heard over the transom that the road was finished. WTF. What's that? Daniel was out like a flash, notified S3 he was going up on the Line to have look-see. Soon he was standing on top of a ridge which had been simply scraped off with a single swipe of a dozer blade just wide enough for one-way truck traffic. Rather than following the flagged alignment compliant with even the most rudimentary military combat engineering standards, instead, the trucks were in plain sight, right on the top of the ridge, traveling all the way to the Guard Post, some half mile away, back and forth. Daniel was livid. Not only had his authority been mocked, doing the right thing had been mocked.

Furious, Daniel stopped the first infantry soldier who came along screaming,
> "What to hell is going on here? I heard the road was already finished and I thought, impossible, way too much grading to be finished that fast, and now I see why! NOW you have done it. No one is safe. Going back and forth will be suicide alley!"

The infantry Private quietly, respectfully and patiently listened to Daniel's rant and then said, "Sir, I think you better tell that to our Company Commander. He is coming this way." The Company Commander, six-foot four football full back type, slowly sauntered toward Daniel in a casual slouched manner that radiated easy authority, saying, "I gave the order to shave off the top of the hill."

Daniel resumed SCREAMING, "Are you fucking CRAZY! You are going to all get killed. They can shoot right at you!"

The Company Commander calmly responded, "Shooting? Shooting? Haven't you noticed. There's no shooting."

                                          Unremembered Victory

Daniel, after a pause long enough to detect whether he could hear shots right then and said, "Hey! You're right. There is no shooting. Come to think of it, I have not heard a shot fired all day."

The Infantry Company Commander said, "'You betcha', Red Ryder. We like riding the trucks back and forth on the road so they can take a shot at us. We particularly like doing it at night with the headlights on. There was a lot of shooting here but not since we started daring them to take a shot. You got us to grade. We added audacity. Between us, it looks like we got Joe spooked good this time. Everybody wins. No one dies. Not even Joe, who's got a mama just like me."

Dan reported the situation back to Battalion and everyone got a good crooked laugh out of the report, trying to visualize the violence they must have inflicted on Joe the first time they did lights-on so that they now the North Koreans were aparently too afraid to take a shot. Then came the thought that Dan liked best. None of these guys were specially selected or trained. No 'A Teams' here; nor Rangers; nor Green Berets; nor Navy Seals. Just guys [and women], pulled out from among us, who met all the enlistment requirments, stood standard training and then put out on a dirt hill facing a lethal enemy and told 'this Line must hold'. That was another thing Dan liked about being out on the DMZ, witnessing ever more evidence of how dying for the glory of your leader was no match for going home with the same free will you rode in on. Tom saw the whole thing, triumph of the ordinary's over the elite.

TO Sir With Love

Lulu, Samantha Mumba

The time has come for closing books and long last looks must end
And as I leave, I know that I am leaving my best friend
A friend who taught me right from wrong and weak from strong
That's a lot to learn, but what can I give you in return?
If you wanted the moon, I would try to make a start
But I would rather you let me give my heart 'To Sir, With Love'

20
TRUTH LONG ASSAULTED FROM EVERY ANGLE
IS YET TO BE DISPROVEN

The news had not made the radio but was stated in Stars and Stripes. A tiny child in Chang Pari, a village right outside the gate of the 2nd Combat Engineer Battalion, was run over by a 2½ ton Army truck. This happened in a combat zone. All civilians were at risk here all the time. All the villagers in the 2nd Infantry Division area were wide open to taking an enemy's bullet as much as a GI. So, what was the big deal of a hapless child of a hapless family playing too close to a narrow road through a village on a dreary overcast late afternoon, in the flicker of an eye, killed by a passing Army truck. Anywhere else, this would be a 'too-bad-move-on moment'. NOT 8th Army. A few days after 2ID reported the incident according to regulation, just as according to regulation, a response came back from 8th Army. The case had been reviewed. No US negligence was found, but, as invited defenders of the Korean People, the 2ID was hereby under orders to offer a sincere and formal apology to the family by the Commanding Officer of the GI driving the truck.

Boy! Colonel Miller was pissed. He really did not want to do it. Daniel was walking by his office when they made eye contact and he got the nod to drop by. The Colonel ranted on about how he just was not going to do it. How he had to get out of it. Someone else can do it, right? Dan was kind of flattered that Colonel Miller was seeking his opinion. It was kind of heady stuff to be in the Colonel's confidence. However, his Cold War School training would not let Dan wander off the reservation. When Dan rolled his eye's the second time and said nothing, Colonel Miller caved. His body, always so erect, slumped down into his armchair. His next comments were about what face to put on this total submission to following orders and what would be best efforts to make the apology acceptable to the heavens.

Not dismissed, Daniel stuck around pleased to get some more face time with his commanding officer. Colonel Miller had been to Dan a steady dependable anchor, holding his world together with the Colonel's calm, steady and human leadership. After some mumbling about getting it over with, Colonel Miller turned to Dan and asked. "Who are these people?

                                    Unremembered Victory

What are they thinking? Hey! You're out there a lot more than I am. What are the KATUSAs like in the field? Hell. Have you seen the enemy? What are they like?"

"Sir", said Daniel, "Everyone on the Line sees or thinks they see human figures dashing about far up ahead, off to one side, me included. But then there was this one time. While flagging the alignment of the road to Guard Post Gladys, I found myself right on the crest of the ridge with MDL markers dead center right along the top. Keeping just south of the markers I hit a highly overgrown stretch of shrub and small trees. Pushing through the foliage, I could not see but inches ahead when, suddenly, a branch pushed aside gave me a glancing view of others present some 200 feet away, north of the MDL Markers. I quickly motioned to my aid, Brune, to stay back. I then slowly pushed the leaves aside again for a clear view of what I knew I was going to see but wanted to make sure was true. There they were. Three North Korean soldiers unloading a truck. More important, that they did not stop unloading the truck gave assurance that, so far, we were not detected. Shifting the weight of my body and inviting Brune to come forward to share our secret view, here is what we saw."

Dan, noticing the Colonel hanging on to every word, went on to say, "Just north of the MDL there was a flat grassy area on their side of the ridge. Nothing else was present other than the truck and some other stacked supplies nearby under tarps. There were three wooden pallets stacked on the ground as we watched them unload a fourth. It was not clear what was in the pallets, most likely canned food.

"All three were in their early 20s, and as you would expect, they looked best-of-breed, being their most best troops from families of the Communist Party Elite, just as ours, as you know, are from families of the South Korea's business elite. Pleased to say our KATUSAs do seem to have a more polished edge over them.

"Back to the enemy, the one in the truck was pushing the fifth flat out the back and the other two had each grabbed a corner. Then, unexpectedly, the one closest to me lost control of the crate and it came awkwardly crashing to the ground. The other two broke out in peals of laughter at the expense of the third, who was clumsily trying to regain his footing and get the box off the ground and on top of other pallets. It did not take long for the third to join the others in mirthful laughter about the mishap.

"As the finished the task and prepared to leave, I motioned to Brune that we had stayed too long at the fair. Time to go." Summing up, Daniel continued, "Sir. They were not only just like the South Koreans. I thought they seemed a whole lot like us, so many of the same gestures and passions and wants."

Colonel Miller bade LT. Schikevitz good night saying, "Thank you Daniel for sharing your encounter with me. Yes. I am starting to see things perhaps a bit better. First and foremost, it's about people, even the enemy are just people. This was good. Thank you. I feel better about how to face the day tomorrow."

The next morning, the Colonel in 'dress greens' uniform was driven to the hooch of the family of the child killed by the truck. The Colonel dismounted the Jeep and walked through ankle deep mud to the door of the hooch. When the Army photographer was ready, he knocked on the door. The door opened. Two women, one apparently the mother and the other the grandmother of the dead child, were standing there. The Colonel bowed slightly in their direction, handed them a formal apology letter, and said, "On the behalf of the 2nd Combat Engineer Battalion, of the 2nd Infantry Division, of 8th Army Command, of US Armed Forces in the Pacific and the American people, we regret a great tragedy that has befallen your family. In performing our mission to defend the Korean People, a US Army Truck accidentally caused the death of your child. We regret this unfortunate loss to your family and community, and I am requesting your acceptance of my personal apology and apology of the American people. Since we believe everyone is created equal, losing your daughter is the same as losing one of ours, a very tragic thing. For this we are sorry. Again, please accept my apology."

The photo was taken and sent to 8th Army as evidence of following orders more than anything else. Stars and Stripes did not cover it. Local Korean Newspapers did. The incident was hardly news since it was strict 8th Army policy to treat every such incident this way. Daniel looked for, but did not detect, any change in the houseboy community or any of the Officer's Club waiters or bartenders. He did sense they knew about it, were appreciative, but expected it. However, few missed noticing this act as but one in a stream of kind acts dictated by 8th Army community relations protocol of making all interests stronger, in the case, starting with the very weakest.

Depending on endearment, rather than domination, for loyalty, Daniel found that the best part of serving in Korea was the seamless mutual admiration between the Korean people and the US Army. Not even a whisper of resentment in the local population. Without question, an immediate payoff for all this kindness was countless North Korean incursions that failed to 'liberate' the South. The North Koreans never found any traction among a people who had clearly chosen to harness their future to free will, no interest in constraint.

SPOOKY
Atlanta Rhythm Section

In the cool of the evening
When everything is gettin' kinda groovy
You call me up and ask me
Would I like to go with you and see a movie?
At first I say: "No, I've got some plans for tonight"
But then I stop
And say: "Alright"

Love is kinda crazy with a spooky little boy like you
You always keep me guessing
I never seem to know what you are thinking
And if a girl looks at you
It's for sure your little eye will be a-winkin'
I get confused I never know where I stand
And then you smile
And hold my hand

21
LIKE AN EXPLORER OUT TO DISCOVER
THAT RAZOR THIN LINE BETWEEN
HOW FAST I CAN RUN DOWN THIS MOUNTAIN
AND THE FALL

It was back in June of '67 when one of LT. Schikevitz's first assignments as Assistant S3 was to review and finalize the design of the Anti-Infiltration Fence. One of his first forays into the DMZ was with Major Timothy Meredith. Perfectly turned out with black oak cluster embroidered in the center of his cap and on his epaulets, Major Meredith was one of those just forty something Majors that left you spellbound in his charisma. It started with his insistence on being perpetually seen with a cigarette in a cigarette holder held in his hand in the most jaunting way, like even better than in the movies. Daniel was completely snowed by his presence and performance. On this bright sunny day in June of '67, Daniel stood with Major Meredith on high ground at the end of a stretch of the AIF already under construction. Their mission was to select, from all the possibilities, the alignment of the next stretch of Fence to extend east through the variegated vacant terrain of the DMZ. Oh yes, the riding crop. Major Meredith was never without it and today he had it out apparently for extra drama when he made his decision.

Though the AIF runs approximately 1 kilometer south of the Demarcation Line, it wiggles all over the place in response to terrain. The Key consideration was fields-of-fire, meaning what mattered most was that every linear foot of the Fence could be observed (no blind spots) from a fortified position as close to the Fence as possible, but just out of range of hand grenades thrown from just north of the Fence.

So back to Major Meredith. He smiled. He looked. He scowled. He just slightly leaned toward a certain orientation and THEN it happened. In a majestic sweeping gesture, his right arm snapped from his side to an extended position where upon his riding crop instantly extended the reach of his hand pointing THE WAY of the next segment.

All present just stared agape at his wisdom in a moment of silence that ended when Daniel asked the Major, "So how far out do you want it to go, Sir?" where upon Major Meredith declared softly, "As far as you can see."

That made Daniel's job easy since his riding crop was clearly pointing to a distinct hilltop a bit over a mile away easily identified on a map. Daniel went back to the Battalion S3 shop and plotted this directive on a map. That stretch of AIF did not waver from EXACTLY where Major Meredith wanted it to be. At the time, no one questioned his decision. All fell in lock step to follow his instructions to the letter. All involved basked in the glow of his confidence and competence, his movement and speech having such engaging charm. The alignment of another one and half mile stretch was done by Major Meredith in the same manner. The rest of the AIF was located by Infantry units assigned to various other segments of the Line who insisted loudly enough that they had a better sense of where to site the Fence for easiest defense than the combat engineers.

A couple of months later Major Meredith was not surprisingly promoted to LT. Colonel, truly a triumph of style over content as you will see. According to procedures, Major Meredith was reassigned to another unit, arriving with his higher rank and authority. Officer's hill was abuzz with adoration and genuine warm feelings for this hail fellow moving on to higher ground. Smiles and salutations abounded. Many were reluctant to leave his going-away party.

Flash forward not quite a year. It's about five months since the Blue House Raid and a lot of the heaviest fighting along the Line was over. As LT. Schikevitz was coming off the Guard Post Gladys ridge road project, he got a new assignment to design an 'elevated fox hole'. Why did the AIF defenses need an above ground fox hole? It turns out Major Meredith, this revered Combat Engineer officer, was totally winging it, making it up as he went along. The problem was that hundreds of yards of these two stretches of the Fence wound up running right down the middle of very large ancient rice paddies that were from 2 to 10 inches deep in water most of the year. The alignments he had selected were totally oblivious to actual conditions. A bigger problem was that he was so universally respected that no one far or near ever questioned, even for a second, his judgement.

Since Dan had extended in assignment three months, as you will see, to get a choice assignment in downtown Seoul, there was no longer a single soul around in the 2 ID who had served under Major Meredith other than Dan. Only he knew the origins of these two segments. It was only when Daniel reconnoitered the areas in question to figure out how to build elevated foxholes that he recollected having never seen Major Meredith ever look at a map. Daniel figured he was just too cool to do that but now, as Daniel saw just how nuts things turned out, he had to admit to himself that most likely Major Meredith could not read a map.

The first response to Major Meredith's design was to position fortifications on the first hint of high ground along the south edge of the rice paddies. However, due to the extents of these inundated flat planes, many of these fortifications were too far from the AIF to observe well enough what was going on. In the heat of battle, this situation had been tolerated, but frustration over multiple successful breechings of the AIF along these stretches prompted a growing desire for a fix.

So how do you build an elevated foxhole? LT. Schikevitz did not even bother to see if there was a such a thing in the Military Engineering Handbook since no such thing had ever been needed before. The first part was easy. You build a strong wooden platform above the highest level of the rice paddy water. How big should the timbers be? That can only be determined after you figured out how many sandbags will be needed to adequately protect its occupants from multiple exploding grenades. That was hard. What are the pounds-per-square-inch pressure of an exploding hand grenade or mortar round? The number existed. With the help of 2ID operations, Daniel found the number. What are the pounds per square inch resistance of one tier of sandbags? Two tiers of sandbags? The numbers existed. With the help of 8th Army operations, Daniel found the numbers.

Plugging these values into structural engineering calculations that Daniel still knew well from university, he came up with the answer: Sandbag walls all around three rows deep, sandbag covered roof 4 layers deep supported by 4 x 16 timbers 2 feet on center. And they built a bunch of them that tightened defenses that led to the day hostilities ended.

SUNSHINE OF YOUR LOVE
Cream

It's getting nearly dawn
When lights close their tired eyes
I'll soon be with you my love
To give you my dawn surprise I'll be
with you darling soon

I'll be with you when the stars start falling
I've been waiting so long
To be where I'm going
There, in the sunshine of your love

I'm with you my love
The light's shining through on you Yes,
I'm with you my love
It's the morning and just we two
I'll stay with you darling now
I'll stay with you till my seas are dried up I've
been waiting so long
I've been waiting so long
There, in the sunshine of your love

Dennis H. Klein

22

1968 WAS THE YEAR WE WENT FROM DEFINING OURSELVES TO BEING DEFINED BY OTHERS

On their last road flagging operation, Tom and Dan fell to talking, with Tom leading off with something that had taken place back at his barracks two nights before. "LT. Schikevitz, that time we talked about what was wrong about the Vietnam War, I didn't really go along with your theories all that much. Now something happened last night that changes all that, though it was just one guy.

Tom went on, "As you know some of the Vietnam wounded are evacuated to Japan for treatment. Once they are deemed physically fit for duty, some are being reassigned to the DMZ to complete their remaining tour of duty here. We had all heard about it, including how for some of these GIs, physically okay, are no longer mentally okay due to whatever they experienced in Nam. Well sir. It's true. I saw it with my own two eyes what a horrible war Nam must be.

"To get on with the story, two nights ago upon returning to my billet to start my day-off, you remember, 24 hours on 24 off, as usual I am bone tired and hungry. I quickly ate dinner, showered and went to bed. The noise in the hooch was mostly the Beatles and guys laughing while playing Partner Spades for a penny a point. Suddenly the door burst open and what had to be the largest man in our unit entered. We quickly learned he had a serious bad attitude: mixture of drunk and angry. No one in the room said a word because in his hand was a gleaming straight razor. He scowled and began waving the razor at no one in particular and everybody there at the same time. He demanded 'What the fuck are you guys doing'? Nobody spoke, but most slowly stood up, trying to figure out an escape route. I was in my bunk at the other end of the hooch pretending sleep but wide awake.

"Sergeant Reed was closest to the angry man and his eyes were wide open as the big man stepped toward him. Suddenly, like a cat, the big guy grabbed Reed and in the same motion had the razor to his throat with Reed's chin tilted upward and the razor shimmering from the lights.

                                   Unremembered Victory

Gilliland said, 'hey man you don't need to do this' to which the big man screamed, 'SHUT UP!'

"I eased my hands from under my covers and looked to my right and there she was, my trusted M-14 rifle locked but not yet loaded. Thank God I had it with me. Moments that seemed like hours passed with the man incoherently slurring his words, claiming that all his problems were the fault of the men in the hooch. Reed was begging for him not to cut his throat and that maybe he could help him with his problem. All we could see was the razor shining and shimmering, a seriously lethal weapon. Reed would have collapsed to the floor if the big man had not been holding him so tightly.

"As quickly as he had grabbed Reed, he tossed him aside causing Reed to fall over a bunk onto the floor. Getting up, Reed carefully grasped his throat to insure it had not been cut as he repeatedly breathed huge gulps of air. It was then I realized my biggest fear – me becoming the center of his attention. Sure enough the big guy looked right at me and said, 'Baker, you motherfucker, I know you're not asleep, get your ass out of that bunk'! He was speaking as he walked toward my bunk some 20 or so feet away. I quickly sat up in my bunk while reaching over for my rifle and released the bolt. That sound had to be sobering. Now it was locked and loaded, and it was pointed right at the big guy. Twenty rounds of 7.62 caliber bullets, a 'full metal jacket'.

"The big man hesitated, and then said straight away, 'Baker, you gung-ho chicken shit motherfucker, you won't use that thing'. Then there just stuff you say at a time like that, as if it had a life of its own, the words were out of my mouth before I knew it, 'Don't make me prove it. Please don't make me prove it." Fellows in the hooch began to move from behind him, to avoid being in the line of fire, because I think they knew and believed I would."

"I told him he needed to leave our hooch right now. At that, he backed out the door never taking his eyes off me. He seemed to have sobered up. He closed the razor and said "fuck y'all, I need another drink". He backed his way out the door and each of the guys peeked out to make sure he had left.

"When we reported the incident, the Sergeant ordered in the M.P.s who quickly showed up. Meanwhile, I went to Captain Chip's hooch to report the incident. He got dressed and we both returned to the Orderly Room finding the M.P.s questioning two other fellows.

"When finished talking to Captain Chip, he took over and ordered the Military Police to find this guy and escort him to the stockade. I was ordered to place one of us at the front of my barracks armed in case he returned.

"So ….", Tom lamented to Dan, "Sir, we really have started something that needs to end fast to cut not just the killed and wounded in action, but as importunately, the mental damage it's causing to all who serve there. Man alive! ALL OVER AGAIN I feel so lucky being assigned to this combat mission that makes me feel more human rather than less.

"Amen to that", said Dan.

Other than light banter, this was the last conversation Dan and Tom would have as they walked off the mountain together. Dan bid farewell to Tom and his rifle squad that had kept them safe on so many missions into about the most dangerous place on earth outside of Vietnam. With Dan going to his new assignment off the Line, neither would see, but not stop fondly recalling, the other again.

23
YOU CAN ACHIEVE ANYTHING
IF YOU CAN MASTER FAKING SINCERITY

The Road to Guard Post Gladys was long complete. The Elevated foxholes were everywhere, and the hostilities had died down to zero, punctuated with occasional stand-out incidents. Dan's time on the line, after 16 months of hostile fire pay, came to an end. His transfer request came in and Daniel was reassigned to the 76th Construction Engineer Battalion, Eighth Army. His title was Construction Project Officer. The job was the biggest troop-construction project in 8th Army history, right at the 8th Army Headquarters Flagpole. This was a real flagpole just outside a complex of redbrick buildings that housed General Bonesteel's offices. The project was a nuke proof, 6,000 SF underground Tactical Operations Center (TOC). Many months before while Daniel was calling around the entire Korean Peninsula, scrounging for some special con-struction equipment to complete a facility along the AIF, he stumbled on to this upcoming project. He secretly put in for it and got the assignment based on discussions with his S3 counterpart at the 76th. They liked his claim that he grew up in a construction family, had poured reinforced concrete since he was 15, got a Civil Engineering degree because his dad was a Civil Engineer. The bad news was that the project would not start for four months. It was April and Daniel would be completing his 13-month tour in May. Daniel really wanted to do this choice project for none of the usual reasons.

When not on the Line, Daniel was back in his billet 'studying' everything, from the arts to literature to history to the sublime or whatever information that he felt would prepare this Civil Engineer for a run at just 'being at Cal'. Along the way, Daniel studied Walter Gropius, founder of a famous modern art school in Germany called The Bauhaus. He stressed that a complete design education requires being the master-builder, directing the construction of a major building from ground-breaking to ribbon cut-ting. Since in Germany in the 20s, this much responsibility was never given to any but the most senior people, Gropius encouraged fulfilling this requirement by acting as the master builder's clerk. Here Daniel would BE the master-builder. He went for it and he got it.

Experience wise, he had already worked every summer and holiday for his dad on huge projects in and near the Washington DC Mall like the New Senate Office Building, East and West Wing of the Smithsonian Institute and the Red Cross Building. Daniel's dad, Irving, loomed quite large in Daniel's life. Daniel was born and grew up in the DC metro, first in a brick bungalow in Silver Spring near the DC Line, or District Line as the locals fondly called it. He would have gone the hottest high school ever, Montgomery Blair, with people in his cohort including Goldie Hawn, Connie Chung, Ben Stein and Carl. You remember Carl. The Woodard and Bernstein Carl. The cultural center of Dan's life was the Silver Spring Hot Shop on Georgia Avenue (just outside the District Line), the cruising capital of the planet. On most hot summer nights, it took almost two hours to drive 4 blocks, one of which was through the Hot Shop parking lot with each parking space offering curbside service. Everyone was there. The greasers with their hot cars and fast chicks, the jocks and their girls all eating curbside. The academics were mostly inside, but by the time you parked and made your way through all the clamor to the front door, you had waved to or been waved at by nearly everyone your age in town.

Nobody was anybody. Their parents typically held a low to a high-mid-level government jobs that paid middle class wages, tops (but the wives did not have to work). Most of the higher paid officials lived in exclusive towns like Vienna and Mclean, south of the Potomac River. Other than well-known doctor families with basement offices in their homes, no one was thought of as rich. Even the upscale homes of the time (they had dens) were quite modest compared to the Mansionetts of Potomac, Maryland that came later. So north of the Potomac there seemed to be no one very rich or very poor, baring the rampant poverty among the African Americans who were only allowed to live inside the District Line. That suddenly changed upon the passing of the Fair Housing act and many who had credit quietly slipped into the suburbs for the first time without incident. Dan's fondest memory of his youth was a universal Silver Spring attitude that …

> 'Something is going to happen, and something is going to happen to me.'

                                                    Unremembered Victory

Now that was all about Silver Spring. Not so with the high school Daniel wound up attending due to the trophy house dad built in Bethesda. Hell. Daniel's family could not even dream of living south of Wisconsin Avenue until a syndicate, led by Harry Yaffee, a HUD housing specialist, quietly bought a derelict country club near the Potomac River and broke it up into 200 housing sites. They sold the parcels to each other to take the real estate brokers out of the loop who only sold to Protestants (this being Maryland, not even Catholics). Called Banockburn Estates, the floodgate was open, but Daniel often wished the family had stayed put. The new High School was like night and day. Your family and situation determined your popularity more than your personality, barring a rare super jock. That was it. There the attitude was …

'Whatever is going to happen to me already has.'

Though Daniel was able to form a fun posse of some four other guys for grins, he spent most of his social life back in Silver Spring at the Hot Shop and Blair High activities, just a 20-minute ride away once he could use the family cars. Unlike Tom, Dan had the resources to hang around the popular Blair High kids, but only marginally, being too far across town.

Waiting for his transfer, Daniel would be serving an extra 3 months on the DMZ, which at the time was hot as a pistol. Being assigned all the most dangerous missions was fine with Dan, having become a bit of a junkie for being in harm's way. Though he could not be sent to Vietnam, he was staring at 11 more months in service back State-side, where nice people were spitting on nice people who happened to be soldiers. Extending in Korea offered other attractive benefits like a three month early out and the total avoidance of projectile saliva. As it was, soon after he got home, at a gathering of acquaintances who had all avoided services, they wholeheartedly expressed how glad they were he was back and how great it would be for Dan to hang with them forever. JUST one small gimme …

'You just spent the last 30 months working for the LA Road Department.
Any other story just won't work for us.'

Soon Daniel left for good for California, glad they fortunately avoided service at a time when perhaps the best service to your country is not serving at all. He would have been one of them if he had found a legit way out of it, something much easier to do as the Vietnam War went on. Daniel went West and rarely saw any of them again.

**HAVE YOU EVER BEEN
(TO ELECTRIC LADYLAND)?**
Jimmy Hendrix

Have you ever been (have you ever been) to Electric Ladyland?
The magic carpet waits, for you. So, don't you be late.
Oh, (I wanna show you), the different emotions
(I wanna run to) the sounds and motions
Electric woman waits for you and me
So it's time we take a ride, we can cast all of your hang-ups over the
seaside.
While we fly right over the love filled sea
Look up ahead, I see the Loveland, soon you'll understand.

24

A KINGDOM IS ONLY AS STRONG AS IT PEOPLE'S BELIEF IN ITS KING
AMERICA IS ONLY AS STRONG AS ITS PEOPLE'S BELIEF IN EACH OTHER

When Daniel reported to his new unit, he found himself in a new kind of war between public universities vs. the private universities. On the very first day he was handed drawings for the underground nuke proof TOC. Shocked, his eye went instantly to just one piece of reinforcement steel every 12 inches on the bottom and the same on the top, holding up six feet of solid concrete, able to withstand a nuclear blast. Dan rejected the design out of hand. He was told that he better be careful what he said and did since the design was the combined wisdom of a Yale graduate architect and an MIT graduate engineer. Further, though all three were First Lieutenants, he was warned that these guys had a lot of say over every aspect of this project and beyond and if he were to succeed, he better be on the right side of them. Daniel met with them and found their combined arrogance breath taking. They could hardly hide their disdain to even have to meet him, a lowly Civil Engineer grad from the University of Maryland. Daniel, as soft sell and as polite as he could muster, explained his opinion was that the roof would cave in upon stripping out the forms, not able to even hold up the 'weight of the beam', much less withstand a nuke. Boy that got them going. They insisted a meeting be held with the senior brass so they could prove to all that their design was just great.

The next morning, Daniel walked into a room already populated with the 76th Construction Battalion Commander and his boss, Colonel McAdo, 8th Army Engineer Group Commander as well as other brass. In the front of the room were the Yale and MIT guys proudly flanking a blackboard filled with equations. Daniel recognized the scribbling instantly and moved slowly but dead-on to the board without looking left or looking right or saying one word. He took his right index finger and rubbed out the number two in the denominator and changed it to a three and the meeting was over. The Yale and the MIT guys eyes got big as saucers for an instant and then quickly looked at the floor to hide their hysteria. Rather than stick around to make excuses for their miss-step, they slinked out the door never to be seen or heard from again. What was the difference. The equation on the board was classic Ferguson's Moment Distribution Across Multiple Supports. Rather than the depth of the slab being cubed, it was only squared. Just saying no to area moment of inertia as basis for structural strength, this little slip made the slab 'exponentially' weaker than their claims, thank you Sir Isaac Newton.

Everyone else in the room gathered around Daniel asking questions and offering cooperation and support going forward. Oh, how lucky Dan was that day. Already designated project officer over the entire operation, Daniel gained full ownership of that title by being challenged by puff.

Then there was the day not too long after that, Engineer Group Commander Colonel McAdo came to the job site while the excavation was under way. Daniel did most of the talking while they walked to the Yongsan Officer's Club. The word was out that McAdo had a shot at a star (General) if the TOC turned out right. It was his decision to build it in-house, mainly as a showboating stunt to bring attention to his leadership. Colonel Macado said little until they sat down across a white tablecloth and he pushed his ample stomach to the edge of the table and leaned over ever so slightly and said to Daniel, "Glad to see you again LT. Schikevitz. Looks like things have advanced well since we first met.

Macado continued, "You know, a project as big as this would typically go on the street for bid and some offshore construction company would just handle it. However, it just struck me a project like this looked doable in-house. I argued with 8th Army that in addition to saving the Army a bunch of money, doing it with troop labor was too good an opportunity to pass up to improve our skill set and to show each other how good we are. Great morale builder. Well they bought it and here you are. I was given an ample buy-in all up and down the Line. All that is left is pulling it off. That puts the spotlight on you. My big question and the reason I asked you to meet with me is to ask you just one question. Can you pull this off without mishap or calamity?"

Macado came off very senior to Daniel, like he was already a one-star general. Big, a bit paunchy with a demeanor that seemed to have a relaxed smile carved into his face that did not match his formal manner. He came off as a man who could handle power but had little grasp of content. That he left to others, by matching the talent at hand to the tasks ahead.

"Sir", said Daniel. "I grew up in a construction family. I can remember for years as a little boy Mom asking Dad at the dinner table every night how many yards of concrete was poured that day. The higher the number the greater the indication of how good a day he had had. I was shooting points with a transit and setting grading stakes with an optical level at 15. At 18, dad got me in the DC Construction Laborers Union, no small task since in DC it's an all Negro. I spent the summer hauling jacks and timbers to set 10X10 column drop heads on the new West Wing of the Smithsonian Institute. It was so hot and humid, I thought over and over I was going to just lose it out there, but I sure learned close at hand …"

At this point Macado, who had been silent, slowly became a bit agitated and blurted, "I Like everything you are saying, but can you pull this off. I mean are you CERTAIN that you can build this TOC on time without a lot of grief?" Interrupted in midsentence, Daniel decided to make his case by finishing that same sentence.

"Sir, as I was saying, after that summer, there was little I did not know how to do personally, like setting wall ties, tying rebar, forming walls and slabs, and pouring concrete, exactly the skills needed to build the TOC. As far as management skills, at the ripe old age of 20, I worked as a field engineer running survey crews and the year after that, Dad started his own construction firm and put me in charge of large concrete pours for an office building and a middle school."

When Daniel stopped to take a breadth, Macado leaned a lot more forward until his nose was about 4 inches from Daniel's and still in a questioning tone, he probed, "So you think you can do it?"

"No sir", responded Daniel, "I KNOW I can do it. Just like with the TOC's design, I was not guessing then! Just like with the TOC's construction, I am not guessing now. I know I can pull it off."

With that word 'off' passing between Daniel's lips, he saw McAdo's tense expression melt into calm relaxation. Macado was satisfied he now had the one ingredient he had no real control over, finding in-the-ranks an officer able to do it. His star in his mind gleamed so large it lit up his face like someone who just hit it big at the slots.

Just to understand how comparatively easy the TOC construction was going to be, there was another not-so-conventional project just some 10 blocks away. The Koreans were constructing a modern-day standard freeway interchange near downtown Seoul, but not with the advantages afforded LT. Schikevitz. The forms were faced with 2-inch bamboo strips backed by a lattice work of small hand-hewn timbers, sticks really.

Daniel was even further fascinated by the native version of a concrete pump. Hundreds of men running up ladders with a 1/3 cubic foot of concrete in a 'chogie bucket' strapped to their backs with a trip lever that opened the bottom. They would climb the ladders, race down an elevated walkway and stop just long enough to have the lever tripped to discharge their load into huge forms. Just seconds to discharge their load, the instant complete, they turned and commenced running once again down another ladder to the concrete hopper, stopping to turn with their backs to the hopper just long enough for a trip lever to drop a fresh load into the bucket and off they would go again.

Daniel had learned in Cold War School that Korean economic planners had run the numbers and found that Korea could develop much faster and further by doing sweat equity (literally sweat) to avoid debt, but more importantly, be better masters of their future, not the international bank that lent the money. Hence, in 1968, that meant using traditional manual methods exclusively. The theory must have worked. Today it would be nearly impossible to find infrastructure as high tech, well-built and maintained as in South Korea.

GOOD MORNING, GOOD MORNING, GOOD MORNING
Lennon, Paul McCartney

Good morning, good morning, good morning.
Nothing to do to save his life, call his wife in.
Nothing to say but what a day, how's your boy been?
Nothing to do it's up to you.
I've got nothing to say, but it's O.K.
Good morning, good morning, good morning, good

25
WHY BELIEVE IN EACH OTHER?
SO, EVERYONE, AS MUCH AS POSSIBLE,
IS ABLE TO DO WHAT THEY WANT TO DO, ALL DAY, EVERY DAY
EXCEPT GET IN THE WAY OF OTHERS TRYING TO DO THE SAME

Daniel had been living at Yongsan in the officer's billets near downtown Seoul, Korea for several weeks when while walking between the closely spaced red brick buildings he was thinking about how quick his reactions had been up on the Line. He remembered how he noticed the smallest detail while on recon north of the Fence - the ruffle of leaves when there was no wind; the slightest footprint; a freshly bent twig; a 5 ft. 7 inch blond, green-eyed figure-to-die-for All American Girl coming around the corner, walking right at him, alone in her Doughnut Dolly outfit with eye contact eminent. Can he do it? Can Dan say 'hello' classy enough so she will say something back?

As casual but affirmative as Dan could muster, he said, "Hello. How are you?"

She responded, "Fine, Thank you, and yourself?"

Daniel added, "The same, thank you" as she passed by him and he saw her pouty lips up close. Daniel just plain lost it as passion totally dismissed reason, "That does it, Daniel thought to himself, 'Amazing my ass. She is surely the prettiest American girl in all of Korea."

The next day, Daniel bumped into another officer whom he had served with on the DMZ but was now assigned to 8th Army. "Hey Daniel", he said, "So glad you made it down. I hear it's still the shits up there but not nearly as bad as before. Got to tell you the Nuke alert was lifted a month ago, mostly due to the Line being so steady. We know it, our families know it, but boy nothing in the press. Why do you think there is such a news blackout?"

Daniel said, "Finally, something I truly know something about. Early on in February, I saw this press truck parked on the side of the road in the DMZ. Everyone on it had PRESS painted on their helmet. Being an officer, I thought, what the hell. I asked one of the reporters on the truck why my parents' letters are so full of questions about my letters that are so full of firefights and guys getting killed, but the Washington Post does not say even one word about it."

Without hesitation, the reporter exclaimed, "We file with AP everyday what is happening but not one word goes out on the wire to be picked up by the papers. No wire, no story. No happen.

"But why is that", asked Dan. The reporter took pause to formulate his words and then said, "The aftermath of the Tet Offensive in Vietnam is such a shock. Our marching orders are the American people cannot handle a second front."

Ralph said, "Hey. You were Top Secret Crypto Custodian, right. Yeah. It goes with your Assistant S3 MOS. So, you knew about Operation Freedom Drop, right. You know, those orders that coordinated Navy Air Force and Army nuke forces IF the Line did not hold. So, you must wonder, why is the news blackout still on long after the threat of invasion is over. Dan had no choice but to respond with a blank stare because it made no sense to him either.

"Oh, by the way", said the other, "There's going to be a mixer of nurses and such tomorrow night at 6 at the Officer Mess patio. See you there?" Daniel said, "I will try."

The next night Daniel attended the festivities in dress khakis. Everyone looked good, most being about 24 and single. AND THERE SHE WAS! The same girl, this time reigning over a coterie of men who apparently had not had a conversation with an American Girl near as her in quite a while, much less the prettiest girl in 8th Army.

Daniel was patient. Finally, he went up to her to make small talk while all the others were kept a strict vigil of her availability. Daniel said, "Hi. My name is Dan. We've already met."

Puzzled, she said, "Maybe? Not sure?"

Daniel urged gently, "Remember, the sidewalk between billets? I said hi and you said hi back."

Linda laughed, "That, was you? I got just a glance. What's your name?"

Daniel said, "My name is Daniel Schikevitz. What's yours?"

Linda said, "Linda McCall, from Ohio."

Daniel said, "I'm from Maryland, surely a more screwed up place than Ohio. Hey look. Seeing how in demand you are, I will be quick. I'm down off the Line. Eighth Army assignment. Maybe I could see you again."

Linda purred, "I am so new in town. I have been here just under two weeks. Great assignment running the main Yongsan Recreation Center. Given how many times I am asked my phone number, I just give it out, so I may as well give it to you too. Boy, those infantry guys are so cute. Oops. Got to go. It looks like that big burly one over there is glaring at me with that look, enough already with anyone else." Linda looked right at Dan for just the shortest second and said, "Great meeting you."

Daniel was grateful for the time he did get, making way for five guys moving in quickly to be the next she talked to. Though there were nurses and other women there, there appeared to be a crowding effect wherever Linda was in the room.

SUSIE Q
Creedence Clearwater Revival

Oh, Susie Q, oh, Susie Q
Oh, Susie Q, baby, I love you, Susie Q
I like the way you walk, I like the way you talk
I like the way you walk,
I like the way you talk, Susie Q

26

**FOR AMERICA TO WORK ALL INTERESTS
MUST BE STRONG ENOUGH TO KEEP FROM
BEING EASILY HARMED BY THE OTHERS
SO BEFORE HE STRONGER TORMENTS THE WEAKER
THEY HESITATED, KNOWING IT WILL NOT BE EASY**

A ringing phone woke up Daniel the next morning. He picked up and said, "Hello who is this?" A voice on the other end said, "Hi Daniel. This is the personnel clerk at the 76th Construction Engineer Battalion. There is an 8th Army Alert. Everyone must go to their mock battle stations."

Daniel said, "What about me. Where should I go. Who do I report to?"

The Sergeant explained, "No one. That is the reason for this early morning call, so you would not be confused by all the clamor. You are TDY. You are to stay put. Constructing the new TOC is too critical to be delayed even ONE second by the rest of the world. You are completely on you own. Do what you want until Monday morning and then go back to work."

Daniel said, "Eye to that and thanks."

Daniel just about did a little jig on hearing the news that every other guy on that base were GONE! and not coming back for a week. Daniel thought to himself, "I cannot wait until 8:00 AM to give her a call, being the only guy in town."

Daniel called her. Right away he heard Linda say on the phone, "Oh hi! I remember you. The Engineer guy I met at the mixer last night. Did you hear the news? BIG alert. Whole place is empty, everyone on maneuvers for a week. Are you still here?"

Daniel said, "Yeah. Finishing the 8th Army underground Tactical Operations Center trumps the alert. Skinny had it that the real reason for this big 'ol super bunker at the 8th Army flagpole is so when things go nuke, General Bonesteel and his daughter will have a nuke proof place to run to."

Linda responded, "Sounds like a darn good reason to me!" Linda giggled. "You must be about the last guy in town."

                                    Unremembered Victory

Daniel offered, "Coffee? The Rec Center. 1:00 o'clock?" "1:00 PM it is." Linda said.

Linda's responsibility was the main Rec Center at Yongsan. Yongsan was an ancient military headquarters complex in the center of Seoul built by the Japanese when they occupied Korea from 1910 to 1945. Japan was in empiric mode then, expanding its tentacles ever further out. As such, the Japanese copied the British Colonialism in all ways including Architecture. No exception, the layout and motif of some twenty billet and office structures in neat rows were solidly in the British Empire style.

As Daniel arrived, Linda said, "Right on time. So, what got you off the DMZ and down into the town?"

Daniel said declaratively, "Oh. I really wanted this assignment. Found out about it as I was nearing going home. A Stateside assignment seemed dumb, not really doing anything and everybody pissed at me for being in uniform. Better I go home sans the uniform. So far, all is going fine. I grew up in a construction family so what's obvious to me is apparently magic to them. So, I will be here until the end of my tour in January. Now about you, it sounds like you've got one cushy job."

Linda said, "Yes. It's true. Yeah. You are right. So far, I have met some of the nicest, smartest, funniest people ever. The only tense moment was the call for auditions for South Pacific we are going to put on next year. The place was just awash with guys wanting to try out. Otherwise, it's so nice. Everyone is so well behaved. Never a fight here. Fights mean the MPs will come. The guys here definitely do not want the MPs to come. As I said, the nicest, most well-mannered soldiers you will find anywhere."

Linda went on to say, "It DOES look like I am facing light duty except for a really big assignment. I have been told that I will oversee the Bob Hope show at my facility in December."

Daniel said, "Yeah, I saw that on the schedule. I will still be here then. Humm. Anne Margaret's in it."

Linda commented, "Should be really something. Hey. Show me that job site of yours."

Daniel said, "I am actually on break now, but we could go by and spy on the night shift after 7:00 PM."

Linda responded, "Sounds Great. Pick me up here. I get off about that time."

Daniel and Linda were walking between two Yongsan buildings that evening when they came to a T intersection at the edge of the project. Here the night became day from spotlights illuminating an impressive construction site teaming with GIs and KATUSAs working together, doing heavy forming, getting ready to pour 18-inch-thick concrete walls the next day. There was a lot of action, 40 workers with two cranes operating full tilt.

Linda said, "Wow. It looks like the roof will be massive, like filling up a swimming pool with concrete."

Daniel said, "Six feet thick with enough steel bar in it to survive a nuke within 1 mile away, just in case the Line were to cave. No contractors. Just GIs and KATUSAs.

Linda asked, "So all this is under your command? You run the whole place?"

Daniel said, "Project Officer, that's me"

Linda playfully fell into Daniel's arms and said, "Good Job." (Code for take me, I'm yours)

The next night in Daniel's billet, a private room with a shared bath, but no one was assigned to the adjoining unit, Daniel and Linda were embracing, their lips meeting for the first time. They kissed hard.

Daniel said upon seeing that the front of Linda's blouse had accidently opened wide, "Hey girl! That's not regulation! As she put his hand right on her breast, and said, "What are you talking about?" as the situation melted into frantic thrashing about.

LOVELY RITA

John Lennon, Paul McCartney

Lovely Rita, Meter Maid,
Lovely Rita, Meter Maid,
Lovely Rita, Meter Maid,
Nothing can come between us When it
gets dark I tow your heart away.
Standing by a parking meter,
When I caught a glimpse of Rita,
Filling in a ticket in her little white book,
In a car she looked much older,
And the bag across her shoulder,
Made her look a little like a military man.

27

RUNNING FAST THROUGH THE ROCKS AND TREES
DOWN THE STEEP WOODED SLOPE
WITH EVERTHING EVER KNOWN BEING DISMANTLED
BY WHAT IS BERING LEARNED RIGHT NOW

About a week later, the alert was over. By this time Linda and Daniel were an item. Each day with Linda grew more amazing and luckier than the one before. The luck did not stop with Linda. As the largest in-house GI concrete pour in 8th Army history neared, Daniel's authority all over town soared, further sparked by 'rumors' about his private life. Concrete pumps for pouring the walls, only two in-country, both on the site two days early. Plywood form wood. How thick? ¾ inch. You bet. How many sheets? 1700 from Japan and on the job site in 2 weeks, the largest assemblage of real plywood in Korean history. Need 220 men to do three-shifts-a-day for a three-day concrete pour so there are no cold joints. All arrived TDY just a day before the pour from all over 8th Army.

Let's go back in time some two weeks after the alert. Dan and Linda were entering officers mess to have dinner. They were making small talk, when Linda suddenly said, "Quick, look to your right like you just saw something interesting. Don't ask, just do it."

Daniel said, "Whoa …" Linda whispered, "It's the Infantry guy again who kind of claimed me nearly the day I got here. He went on alert with everyone else. Really a nice guy, but huge. He's looking right at me. Let's make the turn to the rear tables. He has too much pride to follow."

Once they slipped away and were seated for lunch, and after the prolonged round of just looking at each other, giggling about how lucky they got this far, Linda asked, "So how-to hell did a guy like you wind up in the Army?"

Daniel said, "I ran from the draft for almost my whole first year out of college. I really did not want to go. I mean, I REALLY did not want to go in the Army. It was just something I was not interested in doing. I tried everything after my critical works deferment did not work but eventually, I was doomed. Fighting the draft long enough, I began to feel the entire

                                   Unremembered Victory

American people were looking right at me, making me go in. Raised Southern, Canada, underground or even prison spelled coward. Cal offered me a student deferment but too late. So, I went in and, luck of the draw, some Monte Carlo routine picks me to be here instead of Vietnam and meet you."

Linda said, "But drafted. Bummer." Daniel said, "Yeah. But to soften the blow, at some point I just caved and silently declared (in my head) to the entire 'American People' that if I did not make it home, my blood was on their hands, the whole lot of them. They must have heard me. After the Pueblo was seized and shooting went bang bang on the Line all day and all night, something amazing happened. Everyone on the Line went from 'who cares lollygag bullshit' to 4,000 of our finest fucking GIs, perhaps EVER, wrapped around ME. Well, we are hardly our finest or why was I up there. As luck-of-the-draw nobodies, it was just ordinary us on the Line, backing Joe down, facing the best they have, evidence for me that the ordinary among us is far more amazing than we know."

Dan at this point went into a faux state of rapture. "Oh! Linda! You have no IDEA. You cannot know how much I did not want to go in. I mean like that guy in the song, 'Please Mr. Custer, I don' wanna' go'. And you know I went to Belvoir OCS not to become an officer but just to put off going to Nam 5 more months. Now I will tell you a tale about how America changed all that. At OCS, I am in a barracks with 40 guys in a training platoon, 20 downstairs in two rows of 10 bunks, 20 upstairs. The whole first seven weeks were living hell. You did not sleep. Every night, in the middle of the night, training cadre barged into our barracks screaming that it's time to straighten the bricks AGAIN. They watched over us as we, like zombies, in thrown-on fatigue pants and shirts, went into the dreary Northern Virginia winter night to realign the bricks that made up the drainage ditches around our barracks. They never stopped yelling at us. It was never good enough and we could only feel, not see the bricks, so rebuttal was impossible. Then back to bed for a total of less than four hours sleep and then off to breakfast."

"Not quite. First you took the Army Proficiency test before EVERY Meal. Low crawl 50 yards, throw 5 grenades, did the horizontal bars and ran 1 mile, 4 times around a 440 track near the mess hall. Once in the Mess

Hall, you got to look at food, put food on forks but somehow could not, on command get the fork to your mouths fast enough under the command

"EAT. TOO SLOW RECOVER".

This was mixed in with trivia questions about General Custer and Little Big Horn, like how many died, who survived and other questions about the slaughter. Did not know the answer? Did not eat. Every meal ended in the command, TABLES RISE, whether you had had one bite. It was amazing. By the seventh week I was down to 138 pounds. I looked like a lot of hemp rope."

Dan went on, glad to have a chance to tell his tale, especially to someone who really understood him like Linda. "Clear indication that this brain washing was working was in the fifth week. The emerging group-thought was 'WE HAD TO PASS' the next inspection. There we were on a Saturday morning proud of our perfect gear and glistening barracks. All 40, to a man, started on Thursday spending every spare moment shining boots, buckles, painting equipment so it looked like new. The night before, all were up until just hours before the training officers arrived. The floor was like a mirror. Our beds taught like bongos. Our foot lookers laid out dead on regulation with EVERYTHING dress right dress by the book. We were so shaved head and beard, so sharp and so proud as the training officers entered the barracks and went upstairs. It was not long before we heard them screaming obscenities, soon mixed by the sounds of bunks and footlockers violently thrown against the wall. Soon it was official. The Captain came to the bottom of the stairs and screamed,

"You have flunked the inspection!
Everyone upstairs downstairs.
Everyone downstairs outside. Everyone outside,
DROP! DROP! DROOOPP!"

"So, there I was in my dress greens being ordered, as punishment for flunking the inspection, to low crawl along a drainage ditch full of debris and broken glass, then ordered to do hundreds of pushups. Then ordered to run in formation and when they could tell some of us were about to pass-out, we were given the last order of the day,

'GAS! GAS! You know what that means! Put on your gasmasks!'

"I put on mine and it instantly fogged over until I could see absolutely nothing. Then they screamed at us that no one was told to stop running. So, when we started running in formation again, I got up to a pretty good clip and smacked head-on into a tree, and just before passing out, my only thought was …

"I WANT TO BE AN OFFICER!"

Linda, all twinkly eyed and full of mirth said, "So I guess I am the one who lucked out by you sticking it out, getting your bar, coming here and meeting me." Hey Dan, "Linda went on, "Is it true what I heard right away when I got here that Bonesteel is a smart guy but useless without the superhuman 2nd Division commander, Izenour. We hear he kicked so much butt that they say you can make anything happen in the 2nd Infantry Division but get General Izenour to return a salute. It must be working since the word is that things are winding down, right?"

"Without playing hero, that made it easier to leave the Line. I won't be missed."

Linda curiously enquired, as she so often did, "You act like the guys on the Line are special. You act like they did stuff way over the top. Why do you think Americans are so special? According to your reckoning, if an American has a pulse, they are worthy. Worthy of what?"

Daniel's eyes danced as the conversation turned to his favorite topic, honed to a gleeful edge by his 16 months on the DMZ. "Only Americans are the descendants of the originators of this crazy whirling swirling bottom-up, individual-centered free will shooting gallery. We are the first to just say no to mafia setups and form a state that has no interest other than serving the interests and evolution of ourselves. What an experiment, bottomed on everyone believing in the basic goodness of our collective souls."

"Those Bible people AND the ancient Greeks", witfully said Dan, "They had it so easy living up to their moral codes. Fell behind in the rent. Really could not make it on your own. No problem. In exchange for owed debt, et. al., you became an indentured servant. At the 7, 14 and 21 year mark you were offered your freedom and if you did not take the third offer, you remained a slave all the rest of your days.

"Now, in America. Boy! We're a tough town where even the weakest among us are expected to somehow get though life on their own, whether they have what it takes to pull it off or not. Answer. Everybody else wanting them to make it and, after taking care of themselves, offering a helping hand all they can to get everyone somehow across the finish line. But Linda, that's just me obsessing. I can't stop thinking this way because of what I saw out on the Line, everyone out for everyone else, in this case, of course, to save each other's mortal hides."

Daniel then changed the subject by enquiring, "Enough about me and all my theories. What about you. How did you wind up here?"

Linda said, "It all started when my spineless college boyfriend of three years and I graduated. His parents pushed a Lear Jet on the table IF he would dump me, since his family only marries money and my folks are hardly that. No big remorse. Better to know earlier than later what a jerk he was. But that posed 'the problem.' Living at home with a good teaching job is fine, but in small Ohio towns, IF a single woman stays overnight in Cincinnati or anywhere else, all over town she is a fallen woman. The only way out of the house is matrimony, and the local scene flatlined that hope."

Daniel said, "Confusing. But you are here. How is that if you stuck to the rules?"

Linda explained, "There is an escape valve. In a small Ohio town, there is one way out. Join the military or Red Cross. So, I joined the latter. You go everywhere, do whatever and when you return home and no matter what happened to you while you were gone, you are still considered by the locals as nice a girl as when you left. So here I am. And here we are."

Late that same night, in Linda's apartment, Daniel and Linda were in bed. They had been there awhile, too distracted to turn the lights off. Then there was a knocking on the door and after a pause a second knock and a voice of Linda's earlier Infantry officer admirer saying, "Winda. Are you' in there?"

Quite taken by surprise, practical, level-headed and usually controlled Linda, in a rare surrender to impulse, before connecting ALL the dots, turned off the lights like no one was home. Just as soon as she flipped

                                                   Unremembered Victory

the switch, she knew she had done the wrong thing and as a corrective measure ran back to the bed, jumped under the covers and snuggled up next to Dan and whispered to him, "Oh shit!" as they both continued snuggling, waiting for death.

The infantry officer, having seen the lights go off at the base of the door, though slosh face drunk, now knew she was in there. Slurring his words, the infantry officer said, "Winda, Pweeeze open Up. I wov' you."

Longer pause while Daniel and Linda snuggled together ready for come what may when he burst through the door. Neither made a move to get dressed or any other action than remain snuggled together, too good a feeling to give up just because your end was near. There were more mumbles outside the door that eventually faded away. The encounter left them laughing for days about their bravery and the passion that followed that night, celebrating their survival. The burly infantry officer was shortly reassigned to the Line, not to be seen again.

MRS. ROBINSON
Simon & Garfunkel

And here's to you, Mrs. Robinson
Jesus loves you more than you will know (Wo, wo, wo)
God bless you please, Mrs. Robinson
Heaven holds a place for those who pray
(Hey, hey, hey...hey, hey, hey)
We'd like to know a little bit about you for our files
We'd like to help you learn to help yourself
Look around you, all you see are sympathetic eyes
Stroll around the grounds until you feel at home

28
HEY! NO ONE ASKED TO BE HERE
WE ALL FUZZ INTO CONSCIOUSNESS AT SOME POINT
AND FIND OURSELVES IN A LIFELONG STRUGGLE
BETWEEN OUR NATURAL TENDENCIES
AND THE REST OF THE WORLD

The mutiny came out of nowhere. Relationships between the GIs and KATUSA on the TOC project had appeared normal since day one. Suddenly the KATUSA three-striper approached Daniel and complained, "GI number 10. We NO work. Kajeweski number 10. He gives us shit sandwiches. We no work!"

As the 3-striper finished talking, the 20 or so KATUSA soldiers all walked off the job and stood to one side. It did not take but a question or two and Daniel learned something that up until now had been under his radar. Not only was Kajeweski shorting their sandwiches, he was mocking the KATUSAs when they complained, AND the GIs unanimously, to a man, thought it was kind of funny. Daniel motioned to Sergeant Green, the African American 3-Striper who was really ran this shift, to assemble all the GIs. Sergeant Green said, "Okay. Everyone in the warmup hooch, NOW!"

What happened next was the result of lessons learned in Cold War school. All the GIs sullenly entered the wooden shed. It was dark inside, with just enough light to barely differentiate one face from another. Inside, away from the KATUSAs, Daniel had a little talk with the GIs at the top of his lungs. He started off easy, screaming,

> "Every GI on this site will honor and respect every Korean on this site in all ways and at all times, no exceptions! **THAT'S AN ORDER!"**

This proclamation filled the air with fury long after the words stopped. The complete silence that slowly crept back into the room was deafening as the troops struggled with this abrupt change of protocol. The silence went on and on until Cannon, the Creole crane operator, barely broke it with an almost inaudible mumble, "Sir. You can't give us that order. We're conscripts."

Daniel liked Cannon. He was a solid guy, high some of the time but never even close to hampering his virtuoso top speed crane operations. Cannon's other well-known knack was seeing the world dead on, the way it is. That did give Daniel pause for a nanosecond, but it was the word 'conscript' that set off a flashback. Like it was just happening all over again, Daniel is at Fort Holabird in Baltimore, May '66 being sworn into the United States Army. Everyone in the room was asked to take a step forward. Four guys refused. Just a mere hour later, after a lot of screaming, cajoling and threats, and finally promises they would all get to talk to a shrink AFTER the ceremony was over, all four took THAT step. Back to the moment. Daniel, facing these troops he had grown to cherish as as-good-as-we-get, EXPODED, holding nothing back,

> "WHO HERE did not take **that STEP**?"

This was followed by even a longer silence. Again, Danial screeched,

> "Who here did not take that STEP? There are no conscripts in
> the United States Army.
> Only volunteers!"

A huge long silence that followed was finally broken by Sergeant Green exhaling,

> "Sheeeeeeaaahhhtt."

The mutiny was over. Break was over, and all left the warmup hooch and went back to work. Kajeweska was stripped of his sandwich duties. Before very long, the Koreans started smiling over the change in the GIs' attitude. It was not much, but every GI on the site attempted, to different degrees, to be more attentive to their wellbeing. Then the GIs started smiling, as many do, when they find themselves on the right side of the angels after being jerks. After a while, the whole site was just one big shit-eating grin as their faces melted together into a tight, caring, working assemblage of people.

This really did happen. Daniel only had to lay down the rules once and without any further urging it just took hold and stuck until the end of the project, ahead of schedule, under budget, and with only one busted-open-face-when-a-concrete-pump-coupling bursted. Note, Daniel did not ask anyone to change what they believed, only what they did. Call it phony and superficial but who's to say IF mutual respect (at least on the surface) was made an order long enough what outcomes might follow. Indifference and hate need no orders.

SAY IT LOUD I'M BLACK AND I'M PROUD
James Brown and The Famous Flames

Now we demand a chance to do things for our self
We're tired of beatin' our head against the wall
And workin' for someone else
We're people, we're just like the birds and the bees
We'd rather die on our feet than live on our knees
Say it loud, I'm black and I'm proud

                                    Unremembered Victory

29

YOU HAD TO BE PART ANGEL TO BE ON THE DMZ
IN WINTER OF '68 TO PUT INTERESTS OF OTHERS
SO FAR AHEAD OF YOUR OWN,
FORTUNATELY A TRAIT COMMON TO THE GI NEXT TO YOU

About this time, back up on the Line, Tom entered the Company orderly room to find the 1st SGT pouring over documents on his desk. Top sat in his chair observing Tom before he spoke, "Sorry about the loss of sleep but you still have to go to escort the wood cutters to clear out the new growth around Guard Post Charlie. They are meeting you at 07:30. Get the troops on detail and get after it." Tom looked at Top and said, "You know Top I'm getting really short. Can somebody else handle this?" Top scowled and responded, "That's a negative, we don't have anybody else. You are it, soldier!"

As they set out to meet up with the wood cutters, there were four of them… two new guys, a PFC and Tom. Tom drove the Jeep. He looked over the guys as they introduced themselves. Tom knew the PFC since he was one of the cooks, but the new guys hadn't been assigned yet. Naked sleeve PVT E-2s just newly arrived in the unit. "Shit Turtles", he thought. Tom wondered how this motley crew would instill fear in the enemy? He checked their weapons and ammo and checked to make sure each was ready to be locked and loaded. All seemed in order, so the detail began. Driving with the top off and windshield down made the drive uncomfortable, but there were no complaints as everybody was lost in their own thoughts.

Everything was going like normal until it wasn't…. Tom felt the explosion before he heard it and it lifted the Jeep in the air and all those in it. It came to a stop in a ditch. There was this ringing in his ears. The back part of the Jeep was gone and the two E-2s with it. The PFC was sitting on the ground stunned with blood streaming from a laceration on his forehead. Tom asked, "Are you OK? Can you stand?" Both were disoriented and very confused and Tom's leg was hurting. When he looked down, he saw blood, but quickly realized it wasn't bad…his fatigues were slightly torn. Still stunned but acting instinctively, he grabbed the rifles of the two killed soldiers, pulled the PFC to his feet and started to survey the situation.

Chambering rounds they scampered down into the ditch when the first shots were heard. Dust kicked up around them. They could only guess the direction of the fire but reacted in firing back in the general direction of the sounds. Though Tom he was trained for this situation, he was still bewildered at the suddenness of events.

Tom turned to speak to the PFC when the PFC's face exploded from a projectile expended from an AK47. Blood and brain matter landed on the ground as what was left of the PFC slumped to the ground…. One second, he was breathing, longing for his next beer, yearning for his girl back home, proud of his family and now a lifeless bloody pulp. That did it. Tom felt fear like never before. He was alone facing an enemy that meant him no good. Prone, he rolled over to position himself to return fire when he saw a movement. Without thinking he began to fire and saw a man jerk and fall as three rounds hit his body mass…no more movement from him.

There was no time for satisfaction since he heard a voice speaking Korean giving a command that caused a rush of three or more to run toward him. Again, he fired rounds at all three and again he saw a body fall and then a second body. He jammed in another magazine, not questioning if rounds were left from the first. Chambered a round and fired off again at what he thought was movement. Suddenly incoming rounds were coming at him with intensity. One hitting his foot, and another grazed his head. Blood began to flow into his eyes as he wiped furiously to gain vision. Again, he fired at movement and another body went down. He thought, "how many were there, where are they now?"

Then there was another explosion. He felt the sting of shrapnel that soon turned into burning. He couldn't see, too much blood but he continued firing until the magazine was empty. He realized he wasn't afraid anymore…he was kind of at peace, but he was feeling numb and could feel his thinking ebbing away. The pain was easing, and he felt very tired and sleepy as he thought of home….home and the kitchen stove, his mother's call to get up on Sunday mornings, the fun people next door, the bedroom he shared with his kid brother covered with baseball posters and the girl down the street who was out of his league but not out of his dreams. Struggling, he locked in another magazine but didn't have a chance to fire again as rounds ripped through him…he felt them, but they didn't hurt. Slowly the light was becoming a pinpoint, then fading until he couldn't see or think. All pain and fear were gone. He, the PFC and the two E2s had joined together into nothingness along with the other 100 or so DMZ War dead.

Later that morning, Sergeant Reed came into the orderly and asked, "Top what happened, is it really true about Tom and those other guys with him? Were they all killed? Damn it! Tell me it's not true. Top, it can't be true." The old Sergeant looked up reluctantly and Reed could see moisture in his eyes. This soldier's soldier was visibly upset. He responded, "Anti-tank mine blew up the Jeep and killed two right then, the two new men. The families of the two Privates will get a closed coffin because it will be empty. I can't remember their names…. new arrivals…yesterday."

"The PFC was one of our best cooks, he made all the shit-on-a-shingle we all ate and adored."

"Dang Reed!" Top said, Tom was all right. I had started paperwork to get a waiver, I wanted to get him promoted to E-5. But that is not going to happen now. You know Reed, he must have fought like hell to take four of them before they got him. Terrible. He had wanted out because he was so short and now, he is just plain out. Top sighed saying "Damn!" Boy. He took a bullet for a lot of people out here. Sure, will be glad when this mess is over."

Back down South, when Daniel heard the news of Tom's passing, he was just devastated but comforted a bit by knowing how Tom saw things. Daniel made the trip up to 2ID HQ where he met with Tom's Company Commander to get the address of his family. He also got quite an earful about how Tom was tops, not just an example but an inspiration to everyone in Battalion. His CO went on to say, "How combat ready all the men on the Line have become is lot of Tom's doin's. That guy was real army, but in a citizen's way. He said great stuff, some of it went over my head, but he sure loved America and was glad to face the fire for it. I remember him saying more than once, 'Sir let's go over it again. If I go down, my mom and dad and sisters and brother, cousins, uncles and aunts, all the people on the block, and everyone in town and all the others everywhere get to keep on doing what they want to do all the time. Period. I'm all in.

GET TOGETHER
The Young Bloods

Love is but a song to sing
Fear's the way we die
You can make the mountains ring
Or make the angels cry
Though the bird is on the wing
And you may not know why

If you hear the song I sing
You will understand (listen!)
You hold the key to love and fear
All in your trembling hand
Just one key unlocks them both
It's there at your command

Come on people now
Smile on your brother
Everybody get together
Try to love one another
Right now

Unremembered Victory

30
UNIVERSAL FREE HAPPENS WHENEVER
THE ARTISTS ARE WORKING HARD ENOUGH

THEN, it was HERE. The night before the Bob Hope Show, Linda arranged a sit-down dinner for the inner circle of the show organizers, which was a bit of a small circle; Linda and two others and their boyfriends. Of course, Daniel is Linda's guy and the other was Raymond, Patty's boyfriend, 8th Army Command. Patty was also a Donut Dolly who ran a Recreation Center across town. She set up all the travel and accommodations for the Bob Hope Show performers. Much to Dan's chagrin, Patty had, instead of Linda, a way of being the best-looking American girl in-country among the bra-size-matters-most crowd.

Linda and Dennis and Patty and Raymond had double dated often by then. Dan found Patty a pip. For two whole evenings he listened with patient rapture as Patty went on and on about her hometown of Luvl. How it was the greatest place to be and she was going back, nothing that happened to her out here and beyond was going to change that. How everyone was fun, and the music was special and on and on.

It was the third time they double dated when Patty started up again, but this time Luvl had a huge university with a nationally prominent football team. This put Dan over the top. Feigning mock disdain, he demanded, "Where is this place, THIS LUVL of which you speak so unswervingly? To which, Patty shot back with the biggest, proudest smile and most careful Yankee accent, "Louisville, Kentucky, if you please."

Phil Taska was the one loose guy at the table. He was new in town, assigned to the Naval Command and responsible for direct communications with the show's organization. Phil was just plain charismatic and likable until his intensity started wearing on you, at which point he took derision quite well. Taska just could not stop talking about the big new movie in the States, The Graduate. Anyone who had been in Korea for more than four months could not have seen it because that was at least how long it took for anything to get to Korea. It was like being on another planet, same as earth, just four months earlier than reality.

As much as Taska raved about The Graduate, it took a while to understand what was so special. He explained the scene when 'Plastic' is opined the pinnacle of consciousness. His final pitch was, "It's about one man's quiet rebellion against superficiality, culminating with a would-have-been-conventional bride turning into run-away bride with her lover to nowhere in particular, metaphor for turning our backs on the establishment, striking out on new ground, whatever that is."

Dan asked, "You make it sound like there is a lot of stuff coming down back in the States. Are you saying forget the hippies, even really straight guys are looking at what is going on and saying, 'I'm just not doing it?'"

"Yeah!" said Taska, "You are not being told how busted up things are back home. Here it is almost the end of '68 and the Vietnam War goes on and on, for what! I have to say that '68 feels like a BIG turning point to me. Up until now, ever since Superman got here from Krypton, it has been 'Truth Justice and the American Way'. Now, after all the dumb nasty stuff we have done in Vietnam, we're not sure what we stand for."

At this point, Patty chimed in extending her upper body for emphasis, "I could not agree with you more. We were so slow to fight before. The bad guys had to be really bad. We only got in the right fights; the ones that had to be fought. Now it's 'don't ask, just fight'. No wonder the whole country is busting in two—Those NOT of draft age and those who ARE, and their girlfriends. Boy! Am I one of those!" she giggled.

Daniel added, "Like we are being made into something that we are not by private power that really runs this place by people whose names the media will not disclose by commentators carefully selected according how much they will stay bought. Change the laws back to when we kept the media from being a monopoly. Like, why was I taught in Engineering OCS to embrace General George Custer as my biggest hero of all time. It was all over Ft. Belvoir. 'Serve your nation proud. Be the next Custer. Carelessly take your men into action on your first mission and lose everyone, including yourself. Now that's honor! That is serving your country!' I am not making this up. Worse, I sense this year, 1968, is the year we went from defining ourselves to being defined by others."

                                    Unremembered Victory

Raymond came rolling in proclaiming, "Well none of that shit is going on here. I am five months in at 8th Army and everything I see is straight-up. I look but can find nothing not on the up and up. We support the Line. The Line must hold. We must be an army equal to the task. That is what we do. As for me, Truth, justice and the American way is still alive and well up on the Line and down here at the Flagpole.

Dan said yes to that, telling them his Prokofiev story. He went on to say, "8th Army is starting to feel to me like a tiny remnant of who we used to be while the rest of the military and the Country is turning into something we are not."

Linda, tight on Dan's arm, said "All the more to be grateful we are here. So lucky to get to this safe harbor in one messed up storm. I could have been assigned to Vietnam to do the same job. We've heard that two Donut Dollies have been killed already in combat zones and many of the rest are coming home dark. Night and day and I am so glad I was dealt 'day'!"

"Hey Taska," Dan exclaimed, "I will tell you what the movie-of-the-Year on the DMZ was. The Blue Max. That movie was such a must-see, our Battalion movie theater was packed and full of high drama. Was the Colonel going to attend? He did, only time I saw the old guy there among the troops like that. The movie was just a big ol' shoot'em up standing for nothing but male testosterone and, oh, Ursula Andress."

"Well as for me", said Patty, "the movie of the year in the states was Cool Hand Luke. Got the whole world saying, 'What we have here is a problem to communicate'. Boy does that sums up this whole mess. I never thought my parents could be so easily lead off the reservation. Predatory patriotism I call it, making them feel like they are not good Americans unless they are for the War. Just impossible to talk them out of it."

Taska then added, "Yeah. Thank you, Hollywood for having the good sense to put out Bonnie and Clyde. Gratuitous violence? Not a bad way to intensify these two ultimate outsiders, striking back against an indifferent system. Boy, they got that one right."

"Heat of the Night," said Raymond." This time the Union Army is Sydney Poitier. But like a good American, Syd stands up and the rest back down.

I kind of saw it as Hollywood trying to help everyone really get over Jim Crow, not just legally over it."

Linda added, "That guy Poitier was busy. It was just before Heat, he was in 'To Sir with Love'. Same guy, different setting. Same message. We are all in this together."

Dan then just decided to call it what it is. "One thing is for certain, after 16 months out there, I can tell you there is no color on the Line. Just GIs, one as on the deal as the other, and your damn glad they are there next to you, whoever that is."

Dan went on, "As for me, the Ruskies are a good thing. The Cold War is more a propaganda war than a shooting one. We must be the most attractive people, the ones the rest of the world wants to be like. Russia says they will get to the moon first. No! We are going to get to the moon first! Russia says America is a hypocrisy, glorifying freedom while Jim Crowing a whole chunk of its population. So, thanks to the Ruskies, Jim Crow is being dismantled so we can put our prettiest face to the enemy. Hell, Cold War is forcing us to be part angel, not a bad way to be during a war.

That next morning after the dinner party, suddenly it was HERE. The Bob Hope Show was about to start. Linda was the only conduit between the Bob Hope people and the military. All was seamless as the GIs started filling the seats, a live band got ready to play below stage and Bob Hope, et al, were getting ready backstage.

Daniel said, "Wow. It is really happening. Bob Hope and Anne Margaret too."

Linda said, "Yes, the big day is here. Lots of loose ends starting with my arranging a front row seat for you."

And then it started. Daniel sitting with his knees up against the stage sat back and got ready to see the show, starting with a big-band Las Vegas Review number to warm things up. As the music crescendos, the lights went up and then back down to a pinpoint beam reflecting off Bob Hope's attractive, intelligent, ironic twinkly face that seemed to say 'It's all a joke. Right?' He turns to the center of the audience and said …

"We had a little trouble landing in Korea. They said someone stole the runway."

"Nine-year-old kid tried to sell me a set of luggage. When I asked where it is, he said it was still on the plane."

"Walked down Seoul barefoot. Last thing I remember was paying for the shine."

"I HAD TO COME. The infiltrators are starved for entertainment."

"I visited a soldier in the hospital right after the show I did up north. I asked him if he had seen the show or if he was already sick?"

"Johnson said to Lincoln 'You have a war and a civil rights problem at the same time too. What's your advice?' and Lincoln said, 'Don't go to the theater.'"

"You can always tell when a man's well-informed. His views are the same as yours."

"They have TV here, but the shows come a little late. Lucy and Desi are engaged. Sergeant Bilko is a private. Eliot Ness is still walking a beat. Ozzie and Harriett are expecting. Chester is on the high school track team."

As Hope's jokes flowed on stage, Linda was backstage keeping an eye on everything to make sure it all stayed on track. Despite her official capacity, she could not help playing voyeur, attentively not taking her eyes off Anne Margaret who was clad only in the sheerest slip, steam ironing her silk microskirt dress continuously for six minutes before throwing it on the last second before she hit the stage. Linda then watched from the wings as Anne Margaret, the Anne Margaret! rushed onto the stage as an overwhelming dance landslide of urges and passions. Her moves were strictly hers serving up a delicious amalgamation of the Mash Potato, Twist, Pony, Frug, Jerk, Monkey and the current rage, The Boogaloo. Anne took the popular moves of the day to places they could not go unless she took them there. This pushed Dan into what would prove to be the most meaningful quest of his entire life - taking in and remembering every gesture and sound Anne made, how one followed the other, how big she made us all feel, how it was a celebration not of her, but of us, including her.

She just flat refused to leave ANYTHING OUT.

Just maybe, the Bob Hope Show was, like the 8th Army, a sliver of who we were before Vietnam. Up until '68, each year the nation was swept by a new dance craze, one after the other. Funny, there was no new one to replace the Boogaloo of 67. There never was one again. It all morphed into a sameness. Sure, a few years later Disco came along, manufactured by Hollywood instead of our college campuses. Hip Hop was much later, with no continuity back to the days when American youth, emboldened by their collective power, told the whole world, 'There's a new dance this year and it goes like this.'

A couple of days after the Bob Hope Show, the very atmosphere slowly returned to normal. Linda and Dan whiled away the few days left before his departure. Their time together was coming to an end. There was little talk of remaining an item. The fun give and take on every comment between them; the incredible sex, their physical attraction for each other could not close the gap in their backgrounds. Though both were religiously trained, neither was a believer in anything other than in existence itself. Their relationship had been so sweet to them, existence had to be better for it, making their time together holy as would be their time apart.

About a month before, Linda gave Dan an expensive watch. Dan was puzzled, even confused. He asked why, to which Linda replied, "To remember me by." Dan had finished the TOC. The big concrete pour was over. But for stripping the forms, the job was done. He was relieved of his duties some six days before departure, making it a vacation, able to be with Linda every moment she was not working. At the end, one could say they worked on increasing the richness and intensity of their memories rather than fretting over it ending.

Like the Bob Hope Show, it was here, the last day. Linda was with Daniel at Kimpo Airport. Daniel was waiting to board the plane to take him home. Linda said, "Well here we are."

Daniel grabbed Linda and pulled her tight to him. She started to cry. It was January 7, so it was cold. Knowing he had packed his parka at the

     Unremembered Victory

top of his bag for the flight home, Daniel took off his fatigue jacket and put it over Linda's shoulders. She smiled a smile that Daniel would never forget. He kissed her hard one last time and she kissed him back hard one last time. Daniel was signaled to board the plane. He walked briskly to the plane, turned back at the door, waved, turned again and got on the plane.

Dan changed planes in Japan and found himself the lone soldier on board returning from Korea, the rest coming back home from Vietnam. Dan was particularly wiped out during the next 17 hours in the air, not taking much notice of the hundreds of GIs on the widebody plane. The next morning after the plane landed at Seattle International Airport (Sea-Tac), Daniel found himself in an officers-only staging area being moved about. It was January 8th, 1969. Dan, the only one in dress greens, all the others in summer khakis. Distinctive dress and/or his singular win-ner's attitude among them, he found everyone turning to him like their unanimous leader, as though he knew more than they did about what was going to happen and where to go next.

It was not until well into the bus ride that Dan noticed something he had not seen before - an officer outside without a hat. Dan hesitated and then seeing how friendly the our-of-uniform soldier was with such a pleasant 'with it' face, he asked, "Where is your hat?" Not offended in the least, and with an easy grin, the other officer reported, "I have not had a hat for four months." To which Dan snapped back, "Then we've lost the war?" since, for Dan, collapsed procedures is the flip side of defeat. The other, just as fast, declared with bravado and flourish, as his hand rose from his side to a point off in space, "That thing is GONE!"

It was true. By the end of '68 there had grown a collective understanding that this war was not going to have an outcome of our choice but that of our enemy. Having just experienced further validation that the War was lost, Dan was about to experience real-time, in-your-face ramifications that the Vietnam War was 'GONE!'

Once everyone arrived at Ft. Lewis Washington, they proceeded to Final Pay, a facility right at the gate where each received all the money owed to them in a last paycheck. For Dan, that included much of his monthly pay and all his hostile-fire pay. After signing some papers and receiving a separation check, Dan went out into a sunny parking lot just outside the Ft. Lewis Washington gate to await a bus back to Sea-Tac. That's when it happened – more intense violence than any he had witnessed in 16 months on the DMZ. Years later, Dan had to keep reminding himself that it was JUST January 8, 1969, or 'why wait to have a complete mental breakdown when you can have one right now.'

At first all was quiet. Some hundreds of men in uniforms, a few already changed into civilian garb, were milling about. Here, for the first time in at least two years, each person was no longer a GI but a civilian again. Dan saw on the right side of the sun dappled parking lot some forty men getting on a bus. The parking lot was sprinkled with loose knots of men waiting for their bus and others in a messy line waiting their turn for a cab. Dan's bus was not scheduled to arrive for about another 25 minutes. What happened next, in that short time, was a spectacle that Dan would remember for a lifetime.

It started when a single guy, tall and lanky, hit the lot by himself, screaming obscenities with no rhyme or reason while flailing about taking off his uniform and shoving it in a catch basin. First his shirt, ripping off most of the buttons, one moment it's flung high over his head and the next disappearing into a drop inlet at his feet. The yelling is really getting out there when off goes his pants, then his shoes, socks and then his undershorts, all into the drop inlet. Stark nude, holding his duffle bag in one hand, he violently yanked open the door the first cab in line, with its rightful customers nimbly stepping aside. Yelling at the cab driver to get him out of there, the entire incident is over in a couple of minutes. The parking lot returned to its previous calm, only to be broken again within minutes as two GIs together hit the gate already partially undressed. This time screaming unintelligible obscenities at each other, they frantically stripped down and changed into civilian garb. Quiet returned when they too were soon whisked away in a cab.

Dan was just about all settled down from these two unsettling incidents when the third began. This time, again it was two GIs together, but one was weeping uncontrollably, loudly sputtering stories for the rest of us to hear but too hurried and laced with gibberish to be understood. For the longest time the story went on while the other GI was standing close

                                   Unremembered Victory

by to come to his aid as needed. The two of them eventually got on a bus and left together, but Dan could not stop seeing the anguish on his tortured face and wondered how this happened and thanking almighty existence it had not happened to him.

Oh, how glad Dan was all over again that he had pulled those 'Korean Orders'. Oh, how he fretted in OCS about being fragged in Vietnam by his own men. Oh, how delighted he was at not going to Vietnam. Oh, how his delight became all the sweeter when he wound up in harm's way just the same, facing the fire for his country, but for completely different reasons than Vietnam. Rather than occupiers, Dan saw himself as a guest defender of the Korean people. Rather than distrust by the locals, he had witnessed seamless respect by the Korean People to all things America. No accident, Dan thought, of it as a deserved outcome of 8th Amy's relentless getting-it-right community outreach operations. Dan would forever see the DMZ War as Vietnam turned upside down and driven into the ground like a tent peg.

Compared to what followed in the news, year by year, Dan found his time on the Line, that seemed so ordinary at the time, to become a precious treasure beyond measure. Forever, may those 4,000 randomly selected GIs on the Line be **BEAMING SCREAMING** evidence that, just the way we are,

WE ARE ALL A WHOLE LOT BETTER THAN WE ARE TOLD!

You had to be part angel to be on the DMZ the winter of '68, putting the interests of others so far ahead of your own. Americans have to be part angel to meet the tall order that must be met for there to be America -- Everyone trying to believe in each other, everywhere, all the time, no exceptions. Fortunately, the DMZ War of '68 taught Dan that there would always be enough who are part angel to carry those who are not.

HE END

SOUL MAN

Sam and Dave

Coming to you on a Dusty Road
Good loving. I'v got a truck load
And when you get it, you got something
Don't worry, 'cause I'm coming
I'm a soul man
I'm a soul man
I'm a soul man (come on!
I'm a soul man
And that ain't
Got what I got the hard way
And I make it better, each and every day
So honey, said don't you fret
'Cause you ain't seen nothing yet
I'm a soul man
I'm a soul man
I'm a soul man
I'm a soul man

ABOUT THE AUTHOR

DENNIS H. KLEIN

Dennis' wife says he does not read. He studies. He is a Silver Spring boy and Maryland grad who wound up in California due to a failed critical works deferment from military service. After discharge, he was back, this time at Cal. Though there for a second Civil Engineering degree, he rarely left Wurster Hall urban design studios. He eventually made his stand in '72 with his wife Lynne and three children in Mill Valley California deep in a redwood forest with the Marin Headlands above and a utopic village below, just 18 minutes from San Francisco. After a 15-year career on the front lines of city and regional planning, Klein flipped to geographic information tech services to support the design process and still looks back, using mapping to guide urban policy.

Unremembered Victory was started 20 years ago as a 6,000-word memoir rejected by all the magazines, 2020 and 60 Minutes. Everywhere they loved the story, but it seemed to be red lined as on a never-to-be-told list. As the years went by, Klein discovered to his delight, the book was emerging as a perfect vehicle for sharing the ideas that come him while running the redwoods and meadows of the drop-dead-gorgeous 2000-foot ridge above his house.

Klein did 16 months facing the fire on the Korean DMZ. He remembers many times gladly going north of the Fence at the height of the hostilities because IT HAD TO BE DONE. Ditto, Unremembered Victory. For Klein, the story must be told how 4,000 ordinary guys on the Line in '68 will forever be IRRIFUTABLE evidence that people, just the way we are, have what it takes for us to be America. Because of his time on the Line, Klein believes that nothing can stop him from believing in the whole thing, everything in it, nothing let out, no exceptions, all the time. Unremembered Victory is intended to get you feeling the same.

ACKNOWLEDGEMENTS

WADE THOMPSON

Wade Thompson served in the Army from 1966 through 1969. He was assigned to the Second Infantry Division 1st/9th Infantry Regiment in April 1967. In very early December of 1967 the unit was relocated to Camp Young north of the Imjin River just south of the boundary of the DMZ. In January of 1968 the North Koreans infiltrated the western corridor sector with the intent of assassinating the President of South Korea…, they almost succeeded making their way to Seoul the  capitol of South Korea. Most were killed or captured. Just shortly afterward the North Koreans captured the USS Pueblo and all men on board, with only one fatality.

All units on or near the DMZ were put on highest alert anticipating that the North Koreans would make an all-out assault.

Thompson's unit was in the eye of the storm and the fear and stress associated with the results of such an attack was horrifying. Despite that, the soldiers braced and bonded into a formidable deterrent to the enemy, determined not to give up one foot of ground.

Thompson explains "We were just ordinary guys, but after the Pueblo, became close cohesive fighting unit, each GI giving all that they had to what had to be done. Fire fights were a nightly occurrence with many were Killed in Action and others Wounded in Action. We held firm. We saw not one of our fellow soldiers as heroes, but many…, no most were. We are all proud to have served and done our part in keeping the world from ending in a nuclear exchange."

CHAPTER CAPTION RECAP

1
NOW INCLUDES EVERYTHING UP TILL NOW

2
YOU CANNOT MAKE ANYONE DO ANYTHING,
BUT YOU CAN CHANGE WHAT IT IS THEY WANT
TO BELIEVE

3
WHEN EXISTENCE IS MY ONLY WITNESS, I'M IN
GOOD COMPANY

4
SOME KNOW, FOR SURE, THERE IS TRUTH IN
THE HILLS.
OTHERS CAN ONLY KNOW, FOR SURE, THERE
IS TRUTH IN THE TOWNS

5
" I'M THIRTY, I SAID. "I'M FIVE YEARS TOO OLD
TO LIE TO MYSELF AND CALL IT HONOR."

[THE GREAT GATSBY: F. SCOTT FITZGERALD]

6
ALL THAT IS WRONG IS NOT DUE TO THOSE
WHO CAUSED IT
BUT TO THOSE WHO LET THEM

7
JANIS JOPLIN
"I CAME FROM NOT MUCH BUT LOOK AT ME
NOW. I AM BIG. I AM HUGE.
I AM POWER. IF I AM THIS BIG, HOW BIG ARE
YOU?"

8
… THIS GOVERNMENT, THE WORLD'S BEST
HOPE …
THE ONLY ONE WHERE EVERY MAN WOULD
MEET
INVASION OF THE PUBLIC ORDER AS HIS OWN
PERSONAL CONCERN
[JEFFERSON'S 1ST INAUGURAL]

9
TO DEMAND THE TRUTH, TO SETTLE FOR
NOTHING BUT THE TRUTH,
IS LIKE MAKING LOVE TO EXISTENCE

10
WITHOUT ENOUGH CARING
JUSTICE IS JUST THE STRONGEST WINNING
EVERY TIME

11
ALWAYS STEP IN THE SAME PLACE TWICE
WHEN YOU'RE TRYING TO MAKE A TRAIL.
NEVER STEP IN THE SAME PLACE TWICE
WHEN YOU'RE TRYING NOT TO LEAVE A TRACE

12
FOOD TO THE HUNGRY, WARMTH TO THE
FREEZING
IS GENUINE RESPECT TO THE MARGINALIZED

13
WILDERNESS REVELATIONS ARE NOT SIGNS
FROM HEAVEN.
YOU ARE ALREADY THERE. SIGNS ARE
EVERYWHERE YET TO BE SEEN

14
KIND ACTS TREAT ALL INVOLVED AS OF THE
SAME KIND

15
WHAT ARE THE TWO SPEEDS OF ART?
TRUTH AND WAITING

16
LETTING HATE DEFINE YOU LONG ENOUGH
RUNS THE RISK OF
BECOMING NOTHING BUT EMBODIED HATE
AND YOU ARE NOT THERE AT ALL

17
SINCE THE DMZ DEFENDERS HAD BEEN
RANDOMLY SELECTED,
SWAP IN ANY RANDOMLY SELECTED 4,000
SOLDIERS IN VIETNAM
AND THE RESULT WOULD HAVE BEEN EXACTLY
THE SAME

18
FOUR CORNERS IS A TRICKY SET OF 900-FOOT
HIGH
MEADOW CAPPED PROMONTORIES PLUNGING
DEEP DOWN INTO MUIR WOODS,
GORGEOUS TO LOOK AT, CAN'T STOP GOING
BACK
TO RAVINES SO LARGE THEY KNOW YOUR
NAME,
BUT YOU CANNOT KNOW THEIRS

19
ADVANCE ALL OR SOME AT THE EXPENSE OF
NONE

20
TRUTH LONG ASSAULTED FROM EVERY ANGLE
IS YET TO BE DISPROVEN

21
LIKE AN EXPLORER OUT TO DISCOVER THAT
RAZOR THIN LINE BETWEEN
HOW FAST CAN I RUN DOWN THIS MOUNTAIN
AND THE FALL

22
1968 WAS THE YEAR WE WENT FROM
DEFINING OURSELVES
TO BEING DEFINED BY OTHERS

23
YOU CAN ACHIEVE ANYTHING IF YOU CAN
MASTER FAKING SINCERITY

24
A KINGDOM IS ONLY AS STRONG AS IT
PEOPLE'S BELIEF IN ITS KING
AMERICA IS ONLY AS STRONG AS ITS
PEOPLE'S BELIEF IN EACH OTHER

25
WHY BELIEVE IN EACH OTHER?
SO, EVERYONE, AS MUCH AS POSSIBLE, CAN
WAKE UP EACH MORNING
AND DO WHAT THEY WANT TO DO, ALL DAY,
EVERY DAY EXCEPT
GET IN THE WAY OF OTHERS TRYING TO DO
THE SAME

26
FOR AMERICA TO WORK ALL INTERESTS
MUST BE STRONG ENOUGH TO KEEP FROM
BEING EASILY HARMED BY THE OTHERS
SO BEFORE HE STRONGER TORMENTS THE
WEAKER
THEY HESITATED, KNOWING IT WILL NOT BE
EASY

27
RUNNING FAST THROUGH THE ROCKS AND
TREES
DOWN THE STEEP WOODED SLOPE
WITH EVERTHING EVER KNOWN BEING
DISMANTLED
BY WHAT IS BERING LEARNED RIGHT NOW

28
HEY! NO ONE ASKED TO BE HERE.
WE ALL FUZZ INTO CONSCIOUSNESS AT SOME
POINT AND
FIND OURSELVES IN A LIFELONG STRUGGLE
BETWEEN
OUR NATURAL TENDENCIES AND THE REST OF
THE WORLD

29
YOU HAD TO BE PART ANGEL TO BE THE DMZ
IN WINTER OF '68,
PUTTING INTERESTS OF OTHERS SO FAR
AHEAD OF YOURS,
FORTUNATELY A TRAIT COMMON TO THE GI
NEXT TO YOU

30
UNIVERSAL FREE WILL HAPPENS
WHENEVER THE ARTISTS ARE WORKING HARD
ENOUGH

SIDE STORY: PUEBLO, THE STING

"THE U.S. AT THAT TIME HAD ENORMOUS MILITARY FORCES IN THE WESTERN PACIFIC WITHIN FIVE MINUTES FLYING TIME OF US. I WOULD HAVE THOUGHT SOMETHING COULD BE MUSTERED TO COME TO OUR AID. BUT EVERYBODY JUST FORGOT WE WERE THERE."
[LLOYD P. BUCHER, PUEBLO COMMANDER—AP INTERVIEW 1988]

Years later, Daniel and a long-time friend, Eddy, fellow DMZ War vet, were stuck in a bar waiting to be picked up by their wives, talking about back in the day. Long ago they stumbled on to The Pueblo Incident as a safe common ground topic, rich in subject matter for evoking endless passionate metaphorical exchanges about how they felt about everything. Both had read the Pueblo's Commander's book, Lloyd Bucher: 'My Story'. Both had studied the transcripts of the Navy Inquest Hearings that followed. That the ship got captured without firing a shot is the eternal enigma presented by the state media. You could blame it on ubiquitous lollygag [according to Webster 'fooling around'] that plagued all things military north of Vietnam. You could blame it on something else.

Daniel opened with, "I know I have said it before, and I am going to say it again. You must wonder why Bucher ordered dynamite to scuttle the ship, but it never came. You have got to wonder why he ordered armaments for the mounted 50s, but it never came. And what fool's idea was it for The Pueblo to pretend to be an environmental research ship, out there only to collect marine samples. Any more armaments than the mounted 50 would have blown its cover? And then they put out to sea completely vulnerable, venturing into hostile waters off the coast of mortal enemy nations to track soviet sea, air and electronic transmissions. And THEN, biggest question of all, you've got to wonder why the ship was not put on alert about the Blue House Raid two days earlier, the biggest military event since the Korean War?"

Eddy said, "That's a Roger. If they had been put on alert, those 50s would have been ready instead of under frozen tarps."

Daniel just had to go on, "Now for the big ol' HUGE Why. Bucher was in contact with the 7th Fleet from first citing trouble to when they were boarded. Why was he told that air cover was on the way when it wasn't?"

With mock urgency, Eddy blurts, "I know! I know! Legend has it that no one wanted to have their name attached to the decision to send out planes that could start WWIII, so they kept kicking the can upstairs until someone had enough nerve to wake up President Johnson who DID order the planes, but only in time to see the ship safely moored in highly fortified Wonsan Harbor."

Daniel picked up the story saying, "That may be all true. But how easy would it be to deliberately start this excuse early-on to assure adequately delayed air cover so the ship could be captured?"

And as many times before in these get-togethers, Eddy asked, "And FINALLY, the BIGGER than the HUGE WHY, though the capture took over two hours, so few documents were destroyed, and the Pentagon admits that a North Korean plane flew 900 pounds of paper and equipment, still operational, to Moscow within days of the capture."

Eddy went on, "Yeah. So crazy that it turns out the incentives behind what was going on was not about the Soviet-US face-off, but instead the Sino-Soviet (China-Russia) split coming to an end about that time. It was the Chinese, not Russia, urging Kim Il Sung to heat up the Korean Peninsula, giving and promising more aid for more trouble in the region to best keep North Korea in China's orbit. Don't forget that the DMZ War forced home the crack White Horse and Tiger Divisions from Vietnam, ending any chance of the US winning that war."

"Yeah," piped in Daniel, "But don't forget that the Russians were still stuck with a treaty signed when North Korea was created at the end of WWII obligating them to intervene if North Korea were attacked as though it were their own soil. Not good."

"To me, the funniest part," barked Eddy, "As much as we were scared shit about the Soviet Union starting a direct confrontation with us, that was the last thing Russia wanted. But, help me here, I'm a bit fuzzy trying to remember why."

"That's easy," said Dan. "Just do the logic. No question, 1968 was a VERY GOOD YEAR for the Soviets all over the world. Other than the Dubcek making trouble on their Eastern Front, they were winning everywhere else, gaining followers in Africa, Asia and even closer to us, Cuba and deep incursions into Central and South America. Even Sartre's Paris General Strike appeared to pull Western Europe more to the Russian side. You have got to hand it to Russia. Instead of getting a swelled head, they prudently knew that the last thing they wanted was a shooting war with America to interrupt all this 'progress.'"

Eddy could not contain himself at this statement, as he chimed in, "YEAH and what a twist. The Soviets having no choice but to do whatever they could to keep North Korea from being attacked. Crazy, but remember, behind the scenes they even urged Pyong Yang to release the Pueblo Crew and were told to take a hike.

"Yeah," said Eddy, "I told you before about the 'Meeting in Moscow'. Russia's response to being told to buzz off (as in not returning phone calls over the release of the Pueblo crew). They invited Kim Il Sung to Moscow to offer him a better deal than the one they were getting from Peking."

Dan picks up the story again, saying, "Funny, North Korea sent only a number two guy. Kim Il Sung 'could not get away'. So, what happens? Pyong Yang accepted perpetual Russian subsidies in exchange for ending hostilities with America and South Korea and being in Russia's orbit, not China's, as part of Russia's split with China. Not bad. The cash flow kept coming until the end of the USSR in '89."

"Too many moving parts." said Eddy. "Help me. I've lost it. IF it was China urging North Korea to do nasties like seize The Pueblo or try to kill the South Korean president, where does Russia come in?"

"How soon you forget", said Dan. "Remember the side story. During the late sixties the Russians recruited an American Navy Intelligence mole way up at the TOP who was streaming high end US intel to Moscow. Encrypted, it was well known in the intelligence community that Russia was hot to acquire an American decoder. Who is to say that the ubiquitous I-don't-give-a-shit attitude of the day was used as a cover for the dynamite and armaments not arriving, the ship not put on alert, no intel destruction plan and the fighter jets that never came? Yes. I think you can agree, Eddy. There are just too many what-ifs to offset the high plausibility that the Pueblo was put out to sea to be captured."

Having talked that one out to total agreement, Eddy insisted the strike out on new ground by saying, "Enough about the Pueblo mission being a setup. What about Bucher? Was he in on it? You and I both read his book. We know his character a bit. I say he was. In his own words, with the air cover expected momentarily, manning the 50s would just get people killed unnecessarily. Remember that until the day he died, Bucher, this Boys Town American son, petitioned for a Navy Board of Enquiry on why the promised air cover never came. As you know, he never got it."

Daniel added, "IF he knew the truth, and I think he did, as a good soldier, he kept that secret to his grave to not disclose the deception to the Russians, even after the Soviet Union fell. Only our government can disclose the real reason why the promised air cover never came, not Bucher, and that is not going to happen."

"Exactly", said Eddy, "Here is a man who endured the gates of hell for 11 months of merciless North Korean torture to protect his men as best he could (lost not even one). But after he was cleared of all charges over the opinion of a board of enquiry, why the refusal to respond to his enquiry on why the planes never came, a topic not even touched on the record. I say it was for the same reason, to keep this deception a secret."

Daniel motioned to pause for a moment while he collected his thoughts and then finally said, "If Bucher was in on it, and I think he was, then for the intel's authenticity to not be questioned, someone had to die. Remember, Bucher's final evasive movement was so aggressive he made the North Koreans open fire to stop him from just taking off for the high seas. Killing one, blowing fireman Duane Hodges to bits, and wounding 9 others, including the Commander."

Daniel chimed in, "That make's Bucher the ultimate American soldier. Called upon to take casualties, Bucher, like an artist, worked the enemy to invite hostile fire lethal enough to LOSE JUST ONE, one American, just one being enough to make the intel look real enough to die for."

Eddy smilingly agreed with Eddy, "The man was an artist!"

                                    Unremembered Victory

Daniel then said, "Who is to say that the USSR's long decent into oblivion was not caused by the Pueblo's decoders streaming phony intel that enabled America to lead Russian military spending in all the wrong directions. Oh, how sweet it was to me when their economy collapsed causing the USSR to take its place among the other failed top-down-rules-all totalitarian states. Eddy, I say let's get this version out there. Let everyone challenge all these assertions. Have everyone in the world assault them from every angle. IF it cannot be disproven, then have The Pueblo Sting join the other proud stories of our mainstream American heritage."

Eddy, who had said this before, said it again, "Our Parents, the Greatest Generation, INDEED!"

APPENDIX A
DMZ WAR SUMMARY

Fighting Brush Fires on Korea's DMZ
By Richard K. Kolb

Reprinted from the March 1992
issue of VFW Magazine
With permission

Overshadowed by a more pressing war and largely concealed by Washington, the brush fire war that flared along Korea's Demilitarized Zone in the 1960s went virtually unnoticed by the U.S. public.

Lonely does not begin to describe the campaign waged by GIs in the small strip of land separating South from North Korea. Those infantrymen assigned to the hostile area of operations in the sixties were only a fraction of the total U.S. forces then stationed in South Korea.

Worse yet, their own government refused to recognize the reality of duty on the "Z." Now, over 20 years later, perhaps that recognition will finally be forthcoming. After all, 1991 marked a watershed on the peninsula. On Oct. 4, the last GIs were removed from the DMZ, and on Dec. 12 a non-aggression pact between the North and South effectively ended the Korean War.

That America owes DMZ vets some acknowledgement should go without saying. But this has not been the case, and the men feel it. William Hollinger, an operations officer (S-3) with the 1st Bn, 31st Infantry, 7th Infantry Division in Korea in 1968-69, expressed this hurt in his novel, The Fence Walker.

"If we're killed on a patrol or a guard post, crushed in a Jeep accident or shot by a nervous GI on the Fence, no one will ever write about us in the Times or erect a monument or read a Gettysburg Address over our graves. There's too much going on elsewhere; what we're doing is trivial in comparison. We'll never be part of the national memory."

That theme is a familiar one. Dennis Kulak, who served with the 2nd Infantry Division in 1969-70, put it even more simply. "Being on the DMZ during the Vietnam War was like being in between the proverbial rock and a hard place. Grunts did what had to be done many times without recognition."

Call to Battle

Hostilities on the DMZ were timed to coincide with events in Vietnam. Kim Il Sung, North Korea's dictator, issued his declaration of war in a speech on Oct. 5, 1966: "U.S. imperialists should be dealt blows and their forces dispersed to the maximum in Asia..." Within weeks, North Koreans were probing the DMZ in preparation for a major strike.

That the premier was coordinating his actions with Hanoi's Ho Chi Minh became abundantly clear with the later Tet Offensive and the capture of the USS Pueblo in 1968. For a while, though, the Korean Communist regime was content to send infiltration teams south, wreaking as much havoc as possible.

Their battleground was well-suited for clandestine warfare. Korea is divided at the waist by the 38th parallel. The so-called demilitarized zone runs 151 miles long and is 2.5 miles wide on either side of the Military Demarcation Line (MDL). The MDL is a six-foot wide barbed wire corridor designated by 1,292 yellow markers.

The 'Z', as GIs called it, is not a pretty place. It is a landscape of nightmare, "wrote Hollinger, "this wasteland of a demilitarized zone: artillery craters, barbed wire, minefields, graveyards, the skeletons of villages and the remains of rice paddies. The earth has been shelled, mined, overgrown, booby-trapped, burned and abandoned to grow wild yet another time."

In 1967, a barrier defense system was erected on the southern boundary of the DMZs U.S. sector. It consisted of a Line of obstacles—concertina wire, tangle foot and anti-personnel mines; a 10-foot-high chain link Fence with triple concertina wire on top and six-foot steel pickets driven into the ground; and a Line of towers and foxholes inter-connected by landline and radio.

Of the Fence, Hollinger wrote: "My God, I thought, how can such a thing be beautiful? Its rusted chain links caught the light from the morning sky and the light turned it red, and it became a soaring red curtain rising and falling, following the contour of the hills..."

Ultimately, the 18.5-mile U.S. sector north of the Imjin River and south of the DMZ (an area comparable in size to the District of Columbia) was recognized as a hostile fire zone. Belatedly, in 1968, the Pentagon acceded to reality. A Commander-in-chief of U.S. Pacific Forces memo stated: "The men serving along the DMZ are no longer involved in Cold War operations.

"They are in every sense of the word, involved in combat where vehicles are blown up by mines, patrols are ambushed, and psychological operations are conducted on a continuing basis against Korean Augmentation troops with the U.S. Army (KATUSAs)."

Added to the sheer ugliness of the DMZ is rugged terrain and a severe climate. "The land is incredibly harsh and unforgiving, "wrote vet William Ruskey in Muffled Shots: A Year on the DMZ." In the winter, the winds and ice and snow come lashing down through the mountains from Siberia and Manchuria, freezing the very marrow in one's bones.

"In the summer, the searing heat is sometimes almost indistinguishable from that of a Pittsburgh blast furnace. It is a land where a man can get frostbite and malaria all within the space of a few moments."

Manning the Ramparts
Dating from Nov. 17, 1954, when the Mutual Defense Treaty formalized the U.S. Republic of Korea (ROK) relationship, GIs had been positioned along the border as a deterrent to renewed North Korean aggression. The last of six U.S. divisions departed Korea by March 1955, leaving only the 24th Infantry Division along the Z.

Rotation brought the colors of the 1st Cavalry Division back to Korea on Oct. 15, 1957, replacing the 24th Division on the Line. In 1961, the 1st Cav was the only combat-ready division in the Army. Its 13,000 men were dispersed among 112 camps. Squadrons (about 610 men in each) of the 4th, 9th and 12th Cavalry took turns patrolling the frontier.

During their 13-month tours, cavalrymen spent 193 days in the field. Two weeks of day patrol was followed by two weeks of night patrol. At this time, units were composed mostly of enlistees. On several occasions in 1962-63, troopers were hit by marauding North Koreans.

On Nov. 23, 1962, the 9th Cavalry's A Troop at Outpost Susan was attacked with grenades, killing one American and wounding another. Less than a year later, July 29, 1963, a Jeep from the 9th was ambushed:

                                    Unremembered Victory

two GIs died. During pursuit of the raiders, one U.S. soldier was killed in action (KIA).

Unit colors again changed hands July 1, 1965 when the 2nd Infantry Division returned to Korea to relieve the 1st Cav. Headquartered in Munsan, the famed "Indianhead" Division fielded the 9th, 23rd and 38th Infantry Regiments.

Under the 2nd's operational control was the 2nd Brigade of the 7th Infantry Division, which had been in-country since 1951 and held in reserve since the armistice. A rotation system was inaugurated in October 1967 whereby infantry battalions of the 2nd and 7th divisions alternated duty on the DMZ. "Bayonet" infantry regiments included the 17th, 31st and 32nd.

Two brigade headquarters and five tactical battalions (four from the 2nd ID)—about 4,000 men—faced the North Koreans north of the Imjin River. In addition, "In Front of Them All" in the Joint Security Area (JSA) surrounding Panmunjom, was the 8th Army's Joint Security Force Company.

Attached to each of the U.S. combat units were Korean auxiliaries known as KATUSAs. Issued GI clothing and equipment, these enlisted men (who served three years) provided a direct link to the Korean people. On July 21, 1968, a KATUSA shielded a GI from grenade fragments, earning the Bronze Star.

Confronting GIs on the Line was a highly trained, specialized unit of North Korean infiltrators. The 2,400-man 124th Army Unit of the 283rd NK Army Group trained for guerilla operations in the South. They were lethal adversaries and cut from a different mold than the average North Korean regular.

Stealthily slipping across the border, they carried radio gear, cameras with powerful telephoto lenses and Soviet or Chinese arms. The infiltrator's favorite weapon was the old Russian PPS4 submachine gun, and he was well-versed in its use. He could run for miles with a full load of equipment, expertly conceal himself and negotiate minefields with long steel rods.

A fanatically dedicated communist, the NK would commit suicide with a grenade rather than face capture. "The only thing you find in the morning," said one Sergeant, "is a body with its head and a hand missing."

NKs operated in a world of darkness: infiltrating, ambushing committing sabotage and assassination. Their characteristics and tactics were like those of cousins in Vietnam.

"Joe is not much different than Charlie, "said Special Forces Maj. Roger Donlon, Medal of Honor recipient from Vietnam and commander of the Advanced Combat Training Center in

Korea in 1967." He fights the same way, with ambush, surprise and cunning."

Ambushes were selective, though. "Joe never strikes unless he's got the drop on you, "said one seasoned U.S. officer. "You just can't make mistakes out there or you're as dead as you'll ever be in Vietnam."

Psychological warfare was another NK specialty. It was especially directed at infantrymen manning guard posts at night. Communist broadcast speakers transmitted messages of defection and discontent, constantly playing mind games with GIs along the DMZ, "remembers Dennis Kulak.

"Attempting to turn GIs on KATUSAs, a typical broadcast would be: "Hey GI, look at the man next to you, are his eyes round or slanted? Will he cut your throat while you sleep?"

Life on the Line
To counter NK infiltration, U.S. troops occupied guard posts, patrolled the DMZ and Fence and set "stakeouts." Rules of engagement (ROE) varied according to positioning. Automatic weapons were banned in the DMZ by the armistice agreement but allowed along the Fence.

Also, a clause in the agreement prohibited the use of helicopters on the DMZ." If someone gets seriously hit, it will take us four or five hours to get him out and by that time he would be dead, "said one officer." And don't think the kids don't know it."

A string of United Nations Command (UNC) guard posts (GP), strung along the entire 151-mile front, served as the initial Line of protection. Placed on the crest of 600-foothills, they evoked images of stockades on the Western frontier during the Indian wars.

GPs were circular installments with fighting bunkers extending outward from a circular trench. Bunkers consisted of sandbags and timber. An observation post was in the center. Perimeters were surrounded by two or three strands of concertina wire with Claymore mines staked to the ground with wire.

Each U.S. GP was operated by 10 to 30 men and manned on a 24-hour basis. Normal tours lasted from seven to 10 days. Living conditions were Spartan to say the least. Sanitation and disease-bearing rats were a never-ending problem. Personal deprivation, combined with the constant tension, produced stress, fatigue, fear and loneliness.

Major action occurred at night. Armed only with rifles, M-79 grenade launchers and hand grenades, the men depended heavily on search-lights, flares and starlight scopes. Strange noises—a "groan" in DMZ parlance—often prompted fire." It's a spooky feeling, "said one GI." You always think the groan is Danial Chink—and sometimes it is."

Most significant enemy contact, however, occurred during patrols. Designed to deter infiltration and detect signs of enemy activity, they ran 24 hours a day. Quick fire techniques were stressed to deal with surprises." Hunter-killer" teams, with one man armed with a 12gauge shotgun, prowled the DMZ. Others staked out known or suspected infil-tration routes to intercept enemy agents.

Patrolling the southern boundary, where the decision to fire was left to the individual, was also an eerie experience." Things are sensed or heard before they are seen along the Fence, "wrote Hollinger." You can see nothing, only the mist, and the voices have no source, they are the cries of ghost soldiers raining down from an unseen sky."

In the event the barrier system was breached, mobile reserves were maintained in a high state of readiness. Each battalion had gun jeeps and armored personnel carriers ready to roll. In the 7th Division's area of operations around Tong Duchon and Tok-ko-ri, foot patrols and airmobile searches were employed in counter-guerilla sweeps.

Patrols lasted from a few hours to several days. Moreover, isolated radio relay sites were reinforced by ad hoc security detachments made up of scouts, cooks, supply clerks and medics.

Kim's "Anti-Imperialist War"

Combined, these efforts thwarted large-scale infiltration. Skirmishes with NKs in the post-war '50s were rare. Occasionally in the early '60s a fire-fight erupted, and by 1965 with U.S. engagement in Vietnam, the tempo of activity picked up. Lee Tucker, who arrived in July 1965 to serve with the 2nd Division, remembers "several firefights in which GIs were wounded."

But the opening salvo of the communists' border war began with an ambush south of the DMZ of an eight-man patrol from the 2nd Division on Nov. 2, 1966. With machine guns and by hurling grenades, the NKs killed six GIs and one KATUSA. Each of the bodies were found riddled with bullets, mutilated and bayoneted.

Pfc. David L. Bibee, a 17-year-old, was the sole survivor. Wounded by shrapnel in the leg and shoulder, he survived by playing dead." The only reason I'm alive now is because I didn't move when a North Korean yanked my watch off, "he told reporters." And he almost took my hand off getting the watch."

To save his fellow patrol members, Pvt. Ernest D. Reynolds had launched a one-man counterattack, blazing away at the NKs until they cut him down. Recommended posthumously for the Medal of Honor, the Kansas City, MO native had been in Korea only 17 days before being killed.

Spring 1967 witnessed a dramatic increase in losses due to ambushes, sabotage and mines. From May to year-end, 300 hostile actions in the U.S. sector claimed 15 American lives and 51 wounded. In the first day-long firefight, lasting 18 hours, NKs assaulted a guard post with .30 and .50 caliber weapons.

When the Tet Offensive erupted in Vietnam, Kim took his cue and esca-lated the fighting in Korea. Thousands of Vietnam-destined troops were diverted to Korea in the first months of 1968. The 2nd Division was rein-forced, and tours extended for some of those already stationed there.

Throughout the year, firefights became part of the routine for DMZ grunts. Some 700 hostile actions were recorded. In one action, on April 21, a patrol from Co. B, 2nd Bn, 31st Infantry, engaged a force of up to 75 NKs south of the DMZ. It was perhaps the largest U.S. fight of the border war.

In 1969, action tapered off substantially. Nonetheless, men continued dying. On March 15, a 10-man work party from the 2nd Division was replacing markers on the MDL when it was hit. A patrol sent to assist lost one KIA and 2 WIA. Tragically, seven more lives were lost when the helicopter evacuating the wounded crashed.

The last GIs killed in the brush fire war died Oct. 18. Four men of the 7th ID were hit in a daylight ambush. Their truck was clearly flying a white truce flag. Each man was shot through the head.

As in Vietnam, U.S. forces on the DMZ gradually began to disengage from the front lines." Koreanization" was complete by April 1, 1971 when South Korean soldiers replaced the last 4,000 GIs guarding the DMZ. A symbolic U.S. contingent was left to guard the access road to Panmunjom.

The 7th Division was officially deactivated, after 24 years in Korea, at Ft. Lewis, Washington on that same day." Indianhead" troops moved to reserve positions north of Seoul. For the first time since the end of the Korean War, the ROK Army manned virtually the entire DMZ.

Defending the "Z" cost America 44 of its sons as well as 111 wounded from 1966 through 1969. If the seven GIs killed previously, the sailor from the Pueblo, 31 men of the Navy plane shot down in April 1969 and the seven Americans killed in the '70s are included, the total comes to 90 dead. That's nearly three times the number of Americans killed by the enemy in Grenada and Panama combined.

In addition, the ROK Army lost 326 killed and 600 wounded through 1971. Some 715 North Koreans died in action. Such casualties certainly contradict the notion of the DMZ as a "noncombat zone."

Fight for Recognition

Yet at home, a public numbed by and preoccupied with Vietnam knew or cared little about what was going on in remote Korea. Author William Roskey, a veteran of the DMZ, regretfully wrote: "The old romantic notion of the 'home front' with stars in the windows, a 'stage door canteen', war bond rallies, and support and approval and even sacrifice by those at home died" during the '60s.

Not surprisingly, it was a battle even within the Pentagon to extend due credit to DMZ troops. Hostile fire pay--$65 more a month—did not become effective until April 1, 1968. Receiving it required at least six days a month in the hostile fire zone north of the Imjin River. (Formerly, only the month in which a GI was wounded was counted.)

Standards for the Combat Infantryman Badge (CIB) were stringent: assignment to an infantry company or smaller unit, minimum of 60 days in the hostile fire zone and authorized hostile fire pay, minimum of five firefights and personal recommendation by commanding officer. As one vet was told, "You'll get your CIB along with your Purple Heart."

While these requirements may be justified, the time delineation period is difficult to fathom. Only those who served after Jan. 4, 1969 are eligible. That means those who actually met all the other conditions in 1967 and 1968 are not qualified for the CIB. (The 7th ID created its own unofficial infantry badge featuring a bayonet and division patch in the middle of wreath.)

On the other hand, every U.S. military person who served anywhere in Korea (the entire peninsula, offshore and airspace) between Oct. 1, 1966 and June 30, 1974 received the Armed Forces Expeditionary Medal (AFEM). Americans who faced the same hazards between mid-1954 and Sept. 30, 1966 and since mid-1974, have not been recognized with a campaign medal or ribbon.

As Capt. Wilfred A. Jackson of the 1st Cav's Troop C, way back in 1963, said, "Units serving on the Line (the DMZ) should have and deserve the recognition of the Armed Forces Expeditionary Medal."

Veterans of the various Korea eras have some valid questions about recognition from their government and countrymen. DMZ vets, like their

Vietnam counterparts, "returned to become strangers in their own lad, "felt Roskey, who served in the Z in 1966-67.

Many feel just plain left out. Despite all this, GIs who did a stint on the peninsula since the armistice should be proud, especially the grunts who fought the brush fires on the 38th parallel.

Maj. Vandon Bridge. Jenerette, a 2nd and 7th Infantry Division veteran, said it best: "There are no memorials inscribed with their names or monuments erected that extol their sacrifice. The battles along the Korean DMZ (1966-69) are for the most part forgotten except by the families of the dead.

"However, South Korea now stands as a free country and a phenomenal economic power, given its chance by the sacrifice of those Americans who died there and the thousands who served there."

APPENDIX B
OPERATION FREEDOM DROP

PLAN B IF JOE JUMPS

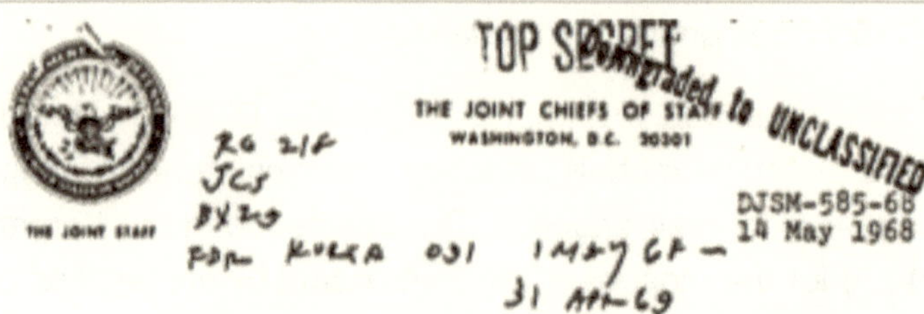

MEMORANDUM FOR THE CHAIRMAN, JOINT CHIEFS OF STAFF

    Subject: Possible Responses to North Korean Attack on the Republic of Korea (U)

    Reference: CM-3223-68, dated 19 April 1968, subject as above.

I. This memorandum is provided in response to the reference and your request for a very informal and brief review of salient features of the contingency plans for Korea. This memorandum provides the current JCS guidance on Korea, the current status of existing contingency plans and their salient features, and a status of actions being taken as a result of the reference. A more comprehensive verbal briefing on the contingency plans is available at your desire.

II. JCS Guidance - Basically the current guidance to CINCPAC and CINCUNC/COMUSKOREA is as follows:

    a. Maintain the Terms of the Armistice Agreement.

    b. Defend Korea.

III. Status of Plans -

    1. Rules of Engagement -

    In support of maintaining the Terms of the Armistice Agreement, General Bonesteel has promulgated Rules of Engagement that provide for the protection and assistance to forces taken under North Korean fire within the DMZ.

    2. CINCPAC OPLAN 27-yr - Defense of Korea -

    a. CINCPAC has recently submitted CINCPAC OPLAN 27-69, which is a complete revision and update of OPLAN 27-65. JCS review, under MOP 144 procedures, has been expedited and will be concluded by 20 May 1968.

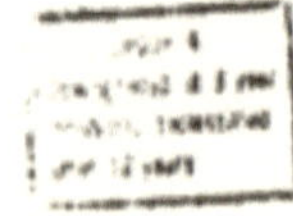

b. Very flexible plan - nuclear and/or conventional - with or without CHICOM and/or USSR intervention - defensive, offensive, withdrawal.

c. Two phases - hold as far forward as possible - when forces and situation permit conduct offensive actions.

d. Forces and Logistics - Force and logistic requirements (up to 12 1/3 US divisions and 40 Tactical Bomber Squadrons) would require disengagement from Southeast Asia, additional force withdrawals from NATO commitments, dissolution of the training base, mobilization, and/or early use of nuclear weapons.

3. As a result of the PUEBLO incident and the deployment of additional aircraft to PACOM to meet the threat of the North Korean air order of battle, CINCPAC was tasked to prepare plans for the neutralization of the North Korean AOB.

a. CINCPAC forwarded his OPLAN FRESH STORM, which has been reviewed by the JCS. Approval will be forwarded to CINCPAC on or about 15 May 1968.

(1) CINCPAC OPLAN FRESH STORM - Four preemptive options and one retaliatory option - conventional weapons - options differ as to forces and timing - round-the-clock operations until North Korean AOB is neutralized or the operation is terminated.

(2) Option ALPHA - US Tactical Air
Option BRAVO - US Tactical Air, ROKAF
Option CHARLIE - US Tactical Air, ROKAF, B-52s
Option DELTA - US Tactical Air, ROKAF, B-52s
Retaliatory - Option ECHO - US Tactical Air,
                                    ROKAF, B-52s

4. Nuclear contingency plan against North Korea - subsequent to the PUEBLO incident, CINCPAC forwarded a basic outline for planning of a nuclear contingency plan against North Korea. A CJCS message informed CINCPAC that his planning concept appeared appropriate and to forward his detailed plan for JCS review and approval. This plan he has termed FREEDOM DROP -

2

a. Coordinated nuclear plan using US tactical aircraft and/or HONEST JOHN rockets and SERGEANT missiles.

b. Three options varying from several military targets to all significant North Korean offensive and logistic support targets - 70KT maximum yield - flexible selection of options or sequential use of options.

c. FREEDOM DROP has been reviewed under the procedures of MOP 144 and approved as submitted by CINCPAC. Message informing CINCPAC of the approval has been withheld by direction of the Chairman, JCS, for a propitious time of release.

IV. <u>Hiatus in Approved Plans</u> -

1. As was recognized, there is, with regard to approved plans to respond to varying scales of North Korean provocative actions, a hiatus between the CINCUNC/COMUSKOREA Rules of Engagement and the CINCPAC OPLANs FRESH STORM, FREEDOM DROP, and OPLAN 27-69 (Defense of Korea). Following is a brief resume of the actions being taken in regard to the reference.

a. Conference at CINCPAC - 26 to 30 April 1968 - developed spread sheets on possible North Korean provocative acts and a spectrum of responses by the United States and/or ROK designed to cause the North Koreans to cease and desist in their provocative acts. These spread sheets and forwarding letter are currently being staffed within CINCPAC's staff and the component commands including COMUSKOREA. CINCPAC has been requested to provide these to JCS by 20 May 1968.

b. The referenced Chairman's memorandum has been released to the Services and a paper has been drafted in preparation for the receipt of CINCPAC's input, at which time the paper will be circulated in the buff. The paper will address possible policy changes required, the delegation and reservation of executing authorities as applicable, and recommended guidance for the preparation of plans, as well as the spectrum of military offensive actions deemed appropriate in view of the possible North Korean provocative acts.

3

 Unremembered Victory

c. As a result of the Pueblo incident and in consideration of possible counteractions and North Korean reactions, the Joint Staff has been working on plans within this portion of the spectrum of options. Agreements among the Services and State Department coordination on aspects of political feasibility have been difficult. The result of these efforts will be included in consideration of <u>b</u> above.

2. <u>Talking Paper for Discussion with General Eisenhower</u> -

a. A Talking Paper has been drafted for use in any planned discussions with General Eisenhower.

b. In view of the present state of General Eisenhower's health, it is believed appropriate that the Talking Paper for your use not be finalized at this time but be held in draft form and finalized up-to-date when your discussion is scheduled.

B. E. SPIVY
Lt General, USA
Director, Joint Staff

4

APPENDIX C
UNREMEMBERED VICTORY

DISCOGRAPHY

"People Got to Be Free" is a song released in 1968 by *The Rascals*. Written by group members *Felix Cavaliere* and *Eddie Brigati*.

"The Fool on the Hill" is a song by *the Beatles*. It was written and sung by *Paul McCartney* credited to *Lennon–McCartney* and recorded in 1967.

"Born to Be Wild" is a song written by *Mars Bonfire* and first performed in 1968 by the band *Steppenwolf*.

"All Along the Watchtower" is a song written and recorded by American *singer-songwriter Bob Dylan*. The song initially appeared on his 1967 album *John Wesley Harding*, and it has been included on most of Dylan's subsequent greatest hits compilations.

"White Room" is a song by British rock band *Cream*, composed by bassist *Jack Bruce* with lyrics by poet *Pete Brown*.

"Jumpin' Jack Flash" is a song by British band *the Rolling Stones*, released as a single in 1968.

"Green Tambourine" is a song, written and composed by *Paul Leka* and *Shelley Pinz* of the *rock* group *The Lemon Pipers*. 1968

"Fixing a Hole" is a song by *the Beatles* that was released on their 1967 album *SGT Pepper's Lonely-Hearts Club Band*. It was written by *Paul McCartney*, although credited to *Lennon– McCartney*.

"My Generation" is a song by the British rock band *The Who*.

"Sad Eyed Lady of the Lowlands" is a song by *Bob Dylan*. First released on the album *Blonde on Blonde* in 1966.

"Stuck Inside of Mobile with the Memphis Blues Again" is a song written by *Bob Dylan* that appears on his 1966 album *Blonde on Blonde*.

"There Is a Mountain" is a song and single by *British* singer/songwriter *Donovan*, released in 1967.

"Dance to the Music" is the second *studio album* by *funk/soul* band *Sly and the Family Stone*, released April 27, 1968.

"Purple Haze" is a song written by *Jimi Hendrix* and released as the second record single by *the Jimi Hendrix Experience* on March 17, 1967.

"With a Little Help from My Friends" is a 1967 song by the British rock band *The Beatles* from their 1967 album *SGT Pepper's Lonely-Hearts Club Band*. It was written by *John Lennon* and *Paul McCartney*.

"Sunshine of Your Love" is a 1967 song by the British *rock* band *Cream*.

"Go Where You Wanna Go" is a 1965 song written by *John Phillips*. It was originally recorded by *The Mamas & the Papas* on their LP *If You Can Believe Your Eyes and Ears*.

"Good Morning Good Morning" is a song written by *John Lennon* credited to *Lennon– McCartney* and recorded by *the Beatles*, featured on their 1967 album *SGT Pepper's Lonely*-Hearts *Club Band*.

"Susie Q" is a song by musician *Dale Hawkins* recorded late in the *rockabilly* era in 1957. He wrote it with bandmate Robert Chaisson. In 1968 Creedence Clearwater Revival recorded it.

"Lovely Rita" is a song by *the Beatles* performed on the album *SGT Pepper's Lonely-Hearts Club Band*, written and sung by *Paul McCartney* and credited to *Lennon–McCartney*.

"Mrs. Robinson" is a song by American music duo *Simon & Garfunkel* from their fourth *studio album*, *Bookends* 1968. It is famous for its inclusion in the 1967 film *The Graduate*.

"Say It Loud – I'm Black and I'm Proud" is a *funk* song performed by *James Brown* and written with his *bandleader Alfred "Pee Wee" Ellis* in 1968.

"Have You Ever Been to Electric Ladyland" is a song by British-American rock band *the Jimi Hendrix Experience*, featured on their 1968 third album *Electric Ladyland*. Written and produced by front man *Jimi Hendrix*.

"Quinn the Eskimo (The Mighty Quinn)" is a *folk-rock* song written by *Bob Dylan* and first recorded during *The Basement Tapes* sessions in 1967. The song was recorded in December 1967 and first released in January 1968 as "Mighty Quinn" by the *British* band *Manfred Mann* and became a great success.

"Ain't Nothing Like the Real Thing" is a 1968 single released by *American R&B/ soul* duo *Marvin Gaye* and *Tammi Terrell*, on the *Tamla* label in 1968

"I Thank You" is a song written by *David Porter* and *Isaac Hayes* originally recorded by *Sam & Dave*, released in early 1968.

"Think" is a song written and performed by American I Thank You. It was released as a *single* in 1968, from her *Aretha Now* album.

NOTE: Musical composition information cited in Unremembered Victory comes from Wikipedia.